ALIEN

WORLDS

Roxanne Smolen

This is a work of fiction and is produced from the author's imagination. People, places, and things mentioned in this novel are used solely in a fictional manner.

ISBN: 978-0-9915673-5-5

Cover and Interior Design by moonRox, Inc.

Published by moonRox, Inc.
Printed in the United States of America

For more books by Roxanne Smolen
visit www.roxannesmolen.com

Table of Contents

Chapter 1

Impani leaned against the tree trunk. She wished she were invisible. A twig snapped, and she bit her lip hard.

Nearby, the beast gave a low growl.

Quaking with dread, she peered around the tree. She saw a bristly black snout and jagged brown tusks. The beast's single eye turned slowly in its socket. It stared straight at her.

With a yelp, Impani took off. She raced through leaves of red and orange feeling as if she ran through fire. Her boots thumped and scarred the hard-packed clay. Her facemask jolted with each step.

She couldn't keep this up. She was fast, but the beast had endurance—and he had it in for her. She shouldn't have entered its lair. That was one of the first rules she learned as a cadet. But the cub was so cute.

Suddenly, her feet flew out from under her. She slid on her butt down a steep slope and landed in a mud puddle. A flock of winged geckos took flight.

The beast detoured around the shallow pool. Couldn't bear to get its fur wet. Maybe she still had a chance.

Spurred by hope, Impani angled back to where she'd forded the stream, leaving her partner, Davrileo Mas, digging up his rocks. If she could reach water, the creature might lose interest. She bounded over gullies and fallen branches. The creature thrashed behind her. It growled as if to tell her it still had her in sight.

Impani stumbled over the uneven ground. Her breath hitched, and she clutched her side.

Thorns reached for her, but her skinsuit slipped through as if she were made of glass. Ahead, she heard the babble of a stream. She forced her burning legs to move faster, arms pumping, teeth bared, and burst from the crimson trees into bright yellow sunlight.

Crashing over the rocky bank, she splashed into the stream. Moisture dotted her mask. She ran until the water was over her knees then risked a glance toward the shore.

The beast paced the bank. Its massive, inward-turned paws raked the rocks. A thick collar of fur stood straight out. Impani gnawed her lip. *Go away. Go back to your baby.* She sighed as the animal lowered its ruff and turned to leave.

An arc of blue-white energy streaked overhead, striking the beast as it lumbered away. With a roar, it reared onto two feet and spun toward the bank.

"No." Impani looked around.

Davrileo pointed his stat-gun and fired again. The blast hit the beast mid-chest. The creature flew back then slammed the ground. Its heavy legs twitched and slashed the air. Impani saw the white of its exposed ribcage, the black, scorched flesh.

"No!" she yelled.

Davrileo shot again. The beast shuddered and fell silent. Impani looked at her partner. She wanted to throttle him, wanted to smash his grinning face.

"What do you think you're doing?" she shouted as she waded across the stream. "It had a cub. It was protecting its young."

"It would have killed you," Davrileo shouted back.

She moved as if to tear at her non-existent hair. "It was *leaving*."

"A little gratitude might be nice," he said. "What were you doing over there anyway? We're supposed to be partners."

4

"We're explorers." She looked at the red and black mass that was once a living creature and thought of the cub alone in its lair. "We aren't here to butcher the locals."

"Well, let's get back to exploring those rocks. This world is a geological haven. I can't wait to give my report."

Disgust seeped into her anger. In a low voice, she said, "If you've cost me my chance—"

She stopped as a familiar tug grasped the pit of her stomach. Alarms wailed in the back of her mind.

They were being recalled. The training session was over.

She usually felt disappointed; she could never learn enough about these distant, alien worlds. But this time she wanted to leave the planet. She wanted to get back to the academy.

Looking up, she imagined a circle of swirling black energy, although she knew the

Impellic ring was imperceptible. She had invented this image of it to calm her fears about traveling through space without a spaceship.

Darkness gathered. Tendrils reached down and pulled her from the world on which she stood. The rocky bank, the sound of water receded. The void enveloped her–deep and empty yet somehow giving the impression of extreme velocity.

Blinding light speared the black. Impani winced. She felt a cylinder materialize at her back, a platform beneath her feet. Her vision wavered then focused upon a mirrored room.

The Impellic Chamber.

Its many reflections showed Davrileo Mas on the other side of the cylinder. Impani removed her mask and slid off the hood of her skinsuit.

"Welcome home, cadets," a voice said through a speaker. "Shower down and report to debriefing."

🪐 🪐 🪐

Impani rushed to Debrief. She found Davrileo and their supervisor, Ms. Kline, huddled together, speaking in quiet tones.

She felt a twist of apprehension. "Sorry I'm late, ma'am."

"Sit down, Impani." Ms. Kline smiled. "Davrileo was telling me about the mineral deposits the two of you found."

Her eyes flicked to Davrileo's face. "Actually, *he* located the deposits. He carried the resonator this trip out."

"It appears that he also secured most of the samples."

"I took samples, too." Impani sat at the table. "I took specimens of trees and moss. And I got a tuft of animal fur."

"I see."

"A planet is more than a lump of minerals."

"True," Kline said. "But when the Board sends colonists to a planet, it's for a specific reason. And often that reason is mining rights. As a Colonial Scout, it will be up to you to assess a world within given parameters."

"But as cadets, we're not *given* parameters. I wanted to bring back as much information as we could."

"You certainly did that." She scrolled down her slate. "You ranked higher than any other team we sent to that world. However, none of them resorted to killing an inhabitant. Tell me about the animal you discovered."

Impani hesitated. "It was two meters tall. Bristly fur. Ran both upright and on all fours. It had one eye, and its head swiveled."

"Extraordinary," Kline said. "This is the first report we've had of a Cyclops creature. A shame it had to be destroyed."

"Yes, ma'am." She glowered. Any points she'd made for finding the beast were now lost.

Davrileo cleared his throat and sat straighter. "My partner was in imminent danger."

"And as partners, you work together, watch out for one another?" Kline looked back and forth at each of them. "I ask because of a discrepancy in sensor readings. Impani, you show an increase in body temperature, adrenalin–"

"I was running from the beast."

"For twenty minutes?"

Impani pursed her lips. Had she strayed that deeply into the woods?

"Yet, Davrileo's readings are peaceful." Kline consulted the slate. "Almost as if the two of you were in separate places."

"Impani wandered away," Davrileo said.

"I wasn't wandering. I was exploring."

"Might have gotten us both killed."

"That's absurd," Impani cried. "You shot that poor thing in the back."

9

"He was coming at you," Davrileo shouted. "If I hadn't shown up—"

"Thank you, Davrileo," Kline said quietly. "You are dismissed."

Davrileo glared at Impani, pushed back his chair, and strode from the room.

Beneath the table, Impani clenched her fists. Heat radiated from her face. She concentrated on gathering her anger into a ball and squeezing it.

Kline said, "Impani, you're at the top of your class. You aced all your studies, and you grasped Impellic theory and logic faster than any sixteen-year-old I ever met. But this is the second report of you leaving your partner."

"I just think you can see more of a planet if you don't keep your nose stuck to an instrument screen."

"Scouting is a dangerous business. That's why Scouts are dispatched in pairs. We'd send you in groups if we could, but Impellic Theory

10

states a ring can transport only two. Otherwise, the ring may become unstable and—"

"I *know.*"

"The point is that you have to work with others. Haven't you wondered why we split the equipment between you? It's so you'll work together."

She groaned. "He shot that creature in the back."

Kline sighed. "All right. You can go."

"No, please. At least, take my specimens into consideration."

"Get some rest, Impani. You're on stage first thing tomorrow morning."

Chapter 2

A hearth dominated the Main Floor Eatery. Spotlights shone upon its station in the center of the vast circular room. Flames shot toward the ceiling. Fingers of mist drew auras about the chefs who danced around the fire.

Impani skirted the perimeter. Her nose twitched at the mixed aromas of multiethnic food. She would have preferred to skip breakfast. The memory of being chewed out the night before still churned in her stomach. But she put on a smile and a better attitude and looked for her friend.

"Over here," Natica whispered.

"Morning." Impani slipped into the crescent-shaped booth. The sides curved overhead, blotting out the sound and sight of other diners. She lifted a glass from a puddle of condensation. "You ordered nectar? What's the occasion?"

"Our almost graduation. And you're late."

"Sorry," Impani said. "I bumped into Mr. Ambri-Cutt in the hall."

"That old raffer. You should remind him that techs aren't supposed to talk to cadets. We can't afford any distractions."

Impani chuckled. "He just wants to show off. He even let me into the control room once."

"If you get caught, you'll both be in deep drel."

A clatter overrode Impani's response. Two chefs collided. A breakfast platter flew. Several daem eggs rolled under a counter.

Her friend grinned. "I love the floorshow here. They're so synchronized."

Impani smiled. Of all the people she had met since her acceptance into the academy, she felt most at ease with Natica Galos. Relaxing against the cushion, she removed the string of emerald pearls she wore draped across her smooth scalp.

Natica picked them up. "These are new. Another secret admirer?"

"They're from that boy who took me to the vids last week."

"Are they real?"

"We can only assume. Whose turn is it to buy?"

"Yours. And I'm famished." Natica tossed the pearls onto the seat then activated the menu. Pictographs hovered over the table. She ordered a boiled daem egg by punching the picture with her knuckle.

Impani studied the floating images. "I think I'll have a sweet cake." She made her selection, and the holographic menu vanished.

"So tell me," Natica said. "How was the session yesterday?"

"It was wonderful. They sent us to a wooded world. The plant life was amazing–deep reds and ocher. Carotene based, not chlorophyll. We would have scored pretty well, except–"

"Here it comes."

"I stopped to look at a cub in its lair. It was so little. Who would have thought its father would be so huge?"

"What did you do?"

"I ran. It chased me halfway across the continent, seemed just about to give up when Davrileo Mas came to my rescue. He butchered the beast on the spot."

"And you think you'll lose points for that?"

She shook her head. "He didn't even try to ward it off."

"Maybe he was afraid." Natica shrugged. "I would have been."

"But to kill it."

"Pani, not every session needs to be spectacular. You're sure to make the program."

"In two days we'll find out." Impani sipped her nectar. She felt embarrassed and misunderstood. The mewling cub came to mind. Did it have a mother to care for it? "How did you do on the physics exam?"

"Passed everything but Impellic Theory. My downfall."

"Everyone hates that subject."

"I'll never get it."

"Sure you will." Impani smiled. "Once I thought a single black hole would devour the universe. But in reality the hole isn't expanding, it's contracting. Along with space and light and time, it's also sucking in itself. Then one day, poof, it disappears and all that's left is an Impellic ring. And what you do is take, say, three of them..." She smeared the condensation from her drink and drew three concentric circles. "The big one powers the other two, and the middle one powers the last. Zips you through space just like stepping through a door."

"If only you were the instructor. You have such a simple way of explaining things." Natica toyed with the pearls. "Speaking of simple, I saw Robert Wilde yesterday. Obnoxious as ever."

Impani hid behind her glass of nectar. "Really?"

"He got a three-day suspension for fighting."

"He's a bully. I don't know why I ever—"

"He says you're in love with him. Are you?"

"No."

Impani set down the glass and looked away. She remembered the night she told Robert she didn't want to see him anymore. He stood outside her room, his face dark and his hands clenched, making her too nervous to fall asleep. She wasn't afraid of him, although she was wary of his quick temper. But lately, she caught glimpses of him in improbable places and wondered if he was stalking her.

A server approached, breaking her reverie. He set their meals before them and retreated without speaking. Privacy was the diner's greatest asset.

Impani sliced the sweet cake into quarters. Dried fruit crumbled onto her plate. "It's strange that in all the time we've been at the academy, we've never been partners."

"Computer glitch." Natica leaned forward and removed the top of her egg. She coaxed out a black tentacle with the flat of her spoon. "I wouldn't mind being paired with the new guy."

"Trace Hanson? Ugh. He's a convict, a common criminal."

"A good-looking common criminal. Aren't you the least bit intrigued?"

Impani pictured him with his legs stretched out before him, slouched in the back of the room. He'd arrived at the academy three months ago and was promptly ostracized, the other cadets whispering. "I've been running from his kind all my life."

"I wonder what his crime was."

"It doesn't matter."

Natica shrugged and ate her breakfast.

Impani pushed her own plate away. "I don't know why they let people like him in the academy."

"They almost have to, don't they? I mean, with the drop in new recruits? Now is the best time to get into the program."

"No, it's tougher than ever," Impani said. "One more incident of lost colonists and they'll shut us down for good. The government needs reliable Scouts to get those people onto safe worlds."

"That's where you and I come in."

Impani smiled. "Right."

Arms crossed, she gazed across the restaurant. How different her life was here—so removed from the warlords and rats, the perpetual darkness of the streets.

No doubt, Trace Hanson came from the same environment. But while she fought to rise above her origins, he obviously carried his with him. Criminal. Convict. She couldn't afford to be intrigued.

They finished their meals, left the Eatery, and stepped into the central tower. A thrill swept Impani as she entered the wide corridor. She would never grow accustomed to the sight.

Gilded archways adorned the ebony walls. Glass-bottomed lifts scaled the heights. Open terraces created a latticework of light bars that merged two hundred stories above. Impani gazed upward as she walked. She wished she could stay forever.

But her days at the academy were nearly over. Natica worried about not making the program, about returning as a failure to her family's dockside fishery on the watery planet of Naiad. Impani had much more to lose. She expected to be executed if she returned home. That was the price she'd paid for freedom—the secret she kept even from Natica.

The tower was peaceful so early in the morning. The silence wouldn't last. Soon the halls would swarm with other hopefuls, chattering and laughing, all vying for a chance to prove their worth. Despite the competition, there was camaraderie among the cadets she'd never known.

She would miss this place. Pass or fail, she would never see it again. Would she remember the academy as being the beginning or the end of her adventure?

With a stifled squeal, Natica caught her arm. She swung her around and pulled her to the side. "There he is."

Impani blinked out of her reverie. She looked where Natica pointed.

Then she saw him. Trace Hanson.

He walked along the far side of the corridor, his gait slow, eyes downcast. He was tall. His shoulders were so wide they strained his tunic. Impani wondered suddenly what it would be like to be held close by those muscular arms.

"You should say hello," Natica said.

"Don't be ridiculous," she snapped, more alarmed at the turn her thoughts had taken than at her friend's suggestion.

Her friend grinned and nudged her. "Go on. This is your last chance. In two days you may never see him again."

Impani squirmed from her prodding fingers. "You're the one who was intrigued."

"All right," she said. "I'll go."

"No!" Impani giggled and pulled her back.

Just then, her gaze met his.

Trace Hanson's eyes were black and deep-set like a hawk. They made her feel he could see right through her, that he already knew her secrets, her faults.

Impani's face grew hot. She turned her back. "Stop it."

"What's the matter?"

"He knows we're talking about him."

"So what? Like I said, this is probably the last time we'll ever see him."

She glanced over her shoulder. He turned down a hallway and was soon out of sight.

With a laugh, Natica linked arms with her and set them moving down the massive corridor. Their footsteps echoed. At last, they reached a huge oblong touch plate in the center of the hall. A holographic roster listed the members of the Colonial Expansion Board.

Natica pressed her palm against the plate's dark surface. Letters appeared over her fingers.

REGISTER GALOS, NATICA H. REPORT TO MEDITATION ROOM 3B.

She smiled and moved aside. Impani took her place. The touch plate acknowledged her.

REGISTER IMPANI. REPORT TO MEDITATION ROOM 8A.

Impani stepped back. "It looks like we won't be partners this time either. I really hoped we'd be together at least once."

"It's a conspiracy. Listen, I have to get going. I'm all the way on the other side." Natica headed for an arched hallway. She called over her shoulder, "Be spectacular!"

"Good luck."

As Impani watched her go, she felt suddenly alone. With a sigh, she entered the hallway leading to the even-numbered rooms. This hall differed from the main corridor. The ceiling was close. Stark lights crisscrossed the pale walls. Instead of polished black tile, the floor was gray and resilient. It muffled the sound of her step.

"Four A, Four B, Six A." At last, she reached room 8A. A green light shone over the door. Impani glanced at meditation room 8B. The light blinked red. Access locked. Her partner was already inside.

She held her palm against the reader. The door slid open to reveal a small room. A couch sat along one wall and a table along another. A non-denominational altar stood in the corner. Light flickered from a panel in the ceiling.

Impani sat on the edge of the couch. She folded her arms, then crossed and uncrossed her legs. The silent altar admonished her. She had no prayers to give.

Be spectacular, Natica told her. She'd have to be spectacular if she were to make the program.

Who would her partner be? Hopefully someone who wasn't afraid to take a chance. Vinod Mouallem would be good. Or Anselmi, the humanoid from the planet Veyt. Anyone but Davrileo. Or Robert Wilde.

Repulsed by the thought, she approached a small mirror and slid the strand of pearls from her brow. She hated that she had no hair. Miserable skinsuits. The techs wanted nothing between her flesh and their instruments. With a derisive sniff, she tugged her tunic over her head.

A line of equipment edged a shelf above the table. Carefully, she took down each piece. From a sealed pouch, she shook out her skinsuit. It was lightweight, finely ribbed with minute sensors and equalizers. She slid her fingers beneath a triple seam and laid it open. The texture was the same on either side. Gathering the suit in her hands, she pushed her foot inside. It molded immediately to the contours of her toes, the curve of her ankle. Slowly, she pulled it up her thigh, keeping the ribbing straight and the fabric even. The tightness eased as the suit adjusted.

She gathered the other leg. Leaning against the wall, she drew the fabric taut along her skin and smoothed it upward to her waist.

Environmental gadgets weighted the sleeves, and she worked her hands into them carefully to position the readers over her forearms.

In front of the mirror, Impani rolled the hood over her naked scalp. She adjusted the insulator band at her forehead, tightened it beneath her chin, then ran her fingers down her body, making sure the triple closure was properly sealed. In her reflection, the seam appeared invisible.

"Done in record time."

Hands on her hips, she turned from side to side. The silver skinsuit picked up the colors of the room as if she were camouflaged. It conformed to her so neatly she could count every rib. So flexible, she felt naked.

She uncoiled her utility belt.

"Hooks and clamps, metallic twine," she whispered as she ran through her supplies. "The refit date on the stat-gun is current. Med-pac is full."

Her gaze fell upon the sonic resonator. She would be in charge of taking scans this trip. Maybe that would give her control over whether she and her partner explored their alien surroundings or just sat looking at pretty rocks.

With a satisfied nod, Impani wrapped the belt about her waist. The latch wouldn't close. *Drel!* She slammed the pin into the buckle and wiggled the clasp. After a few moments, the ready light gave a reassuring blink.

She tossed her clothes into the recycling chute. Fresh clothing would be waiting for her when she returned from the session. As someone who never owned a second set of clothes, that always amazed her. She coiled the strand of pearls and left it on the table where it wouldn't get lost. Then she put on her gloves.

As she turned toward a blank wall, she took a deep breath. "This session will be my most spectacular."

She wiped her hand against her hip then pressed her palm against the wall. A panel slid to expose the Impellic Chamber.

Impani's stomach swooped. Tossing back a mane of phantom hair, she stepped inside.

Mirrors encased the room. They caused the light to bounce at odd angles. A silver cylinder upon a raised dais met its image in the ceiling. There were no computer monitors, no panels of flashing lights—all tech was in the control room. Technicians watched from behind the mirrors.

She crossed the room, sat on the platform, and dangled her legs over the edge. Her partner hadn't left meditation. Leave it to her to show up too early. She swung her legs, feeling the weight of her boots, and saw a hundred images of herself move in sync.

The techs were watching. Would Mr. Ambri-Cutt be among them?

Suddenly self-conscious, she jumped down from the stage and circled the room. The reflective floor hindered her step as if she walked upon the surface of water. Probably the only place in the galaxy where a person didn't have a shadow.

Behind her, the panel from meditation room 8B slid open. *Finally.* With a smile, Impani turned. The smile froze upon her face.

Her partner was Trace Hanson.

Chapter 3

mpani gaped at her partner then struggled to gather her wits. "Hi. I'm Impani."

"Trace." He held out his hand.

He seemed almost shy. Not the brash criminal she expected. She grasped his fingers and offered a tentative smile, but he only stared. Hawk eyes appraised her.

She backed away. All thought scattered beneath the force of his gaze. At the chromed platform, she pretended to adjust her belt while watching his reflection in the mirror.

Trace moved toward the silver cylinder. His skinsuit glowed, outlining his body. Muscles rippled along his arms. He frowned as if deep in thought. Was he thinking of her?

Focus. Be spectacular.

She flexed the hinges on her mask and connected them to the insulator band at her temples. The bulk made her head heavy. She sealed the faceplate and climbed onto the stage.

The room brightened, and her heartbeat rose in response. Soon she would be standing on an alien world. She pressed into the niche along the side of the cylinder. In the mirror, Trace's many reflections did the same.

The light grew to searing intensity. A low-pitched hum rattled her chest. From behind closed eyes, she *saw* the Impellic ring. It spiraled upon itself, trailing black arms like the feeder bands of a hurricane, reaching for her, pulling her from the Chamber. She tensed with vertigo as the ring latched on and spun her into the void.

Just as she thought she might retch, her progress stopped. There was a sensation of flattening against a barrier. The barrier parted.

Impani blinked in the gloaming of early dawn. A breeze patted her back. Sand spread in an endless vista. Dunes scalloped the horizon and edged scattered patterns of tumbled rocks. Nearer, a group of stumpy trees reached like human hands from shadow.

She pivoted on her heels. "It's beautiful."

As if reprimanding a child, her partner said, "We're not here to sightsee. Please run your scans."

"I know the routine." Impani opened her resonator with a flick of her hand. A color-enhanced projection filled the tiny screen. "I'm picking up air pockets in those rocks."

He held a pair of tri-view field glasses to his mask. "They're called caves."

She felt her face redden. "I suppose you're an expert."

"I spent time in a mine."

Of course, she sneered. In the penal colony.

"Your caves are the only point of interest." He folded the glasses and hooked them to his belt. "It will be a bit of a hike to get there."

She stretched out her arms and danced. "We're in the middle of a desert. It's going to be a hike to get anywhere."

With a curt nod, he headed toward the rocks.

Killjoy. He has no sense of wonder.

She checked the environmental sensors upon her sleeve. The readings shone green—oxygen normal. Raising her mask upon its hinges, she breathed deeply of the alien air. The breeze was hot and dry, rich with spicy overtones.

She slid the mask until it rested upon her head then hurried to catch her partner. "I smell sage."

He glanced at her and increased his pace. "We haven't tested the atmosphere, Impani."

"We're students. They wouldn't send us to a toxic world."

"Mistakes happen."

With a shrug, she fell silent–then smiled when, after a moment, he lifted his own mask.

They trudged through the sand to the trees. Up close, they looked even more like wretched hands–the bark smooth and pale, limbs thick and bent. In the palm of one, she found the stringy remains of a bird's nest and two broken eggshells, each the size of her thumbnail. She sealed a sample of the shell in a specimen container.

A gust of wind peppered them with grit. Bands of light brought muted color to the sky.

"Do you suppose this entire planet is a desert?" she asked.

"It would make sense. That way each team would be up against the same conditions."

Impani thought of the other students scattered in pairs across the planet's surface, each trying to out-do the next. She skipped ahead to face her partner, walking backward. "I have an idea. Let's not search the caves."

"Why?"

"Because it's expected. Because every recruit of every session before us must have searched those caves. I want to do something spectacular. I want to see what's over that rise."

"Absolutely not. We're Scouts, not tourists. If we're expected to search the caves, then that's what we should do."

"We're not Scouts yet, and we never will be if we don't show them we can take a chance."

Trace walked on.

She trotted after him. "Look, what's the point of these testing sessions? To scout out as much of the planet as possible and to report something that has never been seen before, right? Well, we aren't going to do that from inside a cave that's obviously been set up as a first stop."

"This is a desert. We could walk for hours and not see anything."

"That's where the part about taking a chance comes in, but Trace… Trace!"

With a growl, he threw his hands into the air. He walked away with exaggerated gestures.

Impani kicked the sand and glared at his back. He was impossible. He had no daring, no love of adventure. How could he have been promoted to her class in just three months?

Turning toward the sunrise, she squinted into the light. What was beyond the stretch of open land?

Trace felt the thud of his boots as he stormed over the uneven sand. He should pace himself, but at that moment, all he wanted was to get away from his partner. She was reckless, heedless. An obvious troublemaker. Right when he needed to prove he could be a model Scout.

The first time he saw Impani, he'd bumped into her in the doorway of the Astrophysics Lab. Her eyes were so bright a shade of green they'd startled him. She wore an expensive piece of jewelry across her forehead.

Obviously, she was rich. He'd known many rich girls—empty headed and trite. They treated him as if he were a prize, or worse, as if he was incidental.

All they wanted was his family's land. His father couldn't see it, hosting affair after gala affair, trying to trap him with matrimony. He wanted his only son to remain at the plantation and manage the family holdings.

But Trace was barely seventeen years old. He wanted to see the galaxy, not settle down into a loveless marriage. That as much as anything had led him to run away from home and take a job as an off-loader on the Umiak.

A rash decision. Look what became of it.

He scowled at the memory and lengthened his stride. Shadows grew before him. They accented the dips and swirls of sand as the scorching sunlight strengthened at his back.

His father would adore Impani. Beautiful. Vain. Stubborn. The problem was she was right. All the previous scouting teams would have investigated the caves. He doubted they would find anything of interest there.

He would improvise. He'd prove to the Board that he could succeed, that they were right to take a chance on him. His only alternative was prison.

Trace leaned into a gust of wind and walked away from his partner.

≈ ≈ ≈

Impani faced the rising sun. She was wasting time. No one would blame her if she headed toward the rise alone.

Or would they? In Ms. Kline's debriefing yesterday, Davrileo Mas reported that she'd wandered away and had to be rescued. If she walked off again, would she be labeled a loner, someone who didn't work well with others? Would she be dropped from the program?

Her shoulders sank. She'd come too far to risk everything now. She would have to make amends, try to salvage the session. She turned and looked for her partner.

Trace Hanson was a silhouette. Distant and dark. He had not slackened his pace waiting for her. Beyond him, naked boulders gleamed white against their shadow like the bones of the desert.

Impani rushed to catch up. By the time she reached him, she was panting.

"You were right about the hike. My legs are tired." She paused for an answer then continued upon his silence. "Will you do one thing for me? Before we crawl into your caves, can we climb to the top of the rocks for a minute, just to look around?"

Trace walked briskly. Impani listened to the quickness of his breath. All around, dunes rose and fell in silent monotony.

She said, "How about if I do all the climbing?"

Just then, an animal stepped from behind the rocks. It stood at least a meter and a half at the shoulder and had thick, shaggy fur.

The two cadets froze.

As if unimpressed by them, the creature turned its back. It walked along the line of rocks with its wide muzzle nuzzling each crevice. Its snorts stirred the loose sand.

Trace whispered, "Take the safety off your stat-gun. In case it attacks."

"No. We're not here to butcher the locals. Let's approach slowly. Show it we can be friends."

Neither one moved.

She nudged him. "Go on. It has hooves. It doesn't eat meat."

"Perhaps it's not aware of that rule." He glanced behind them as if plotting a course back to the trees.

Time to take a chance. She stepped forward.

The bovine head lifted. Large eyes regarded her from beneath a heavy fringe of lashes. It exhaled loudly. She tensed, awaiting the animal's charge; but it never came. They studied each other in silence. After a moment, the beast turned away and continued to root.

What was it looking for? Impani craned her neck. A slender purple flower poked out of the sand. The animal snapped up the blossom. Great cloven feet moved the sand away to expose hidden tubers.

"Plant life." Trace appeared beside her. "Your friend may be vegetarian after all."

A rush of adrenaline coursed through her. "My friend is going to help us tour the desert."

"What? Impani, wait!"

Impani crept nearer. The animal raised its head. She held out her hand and stood so close she could touch its nose. It snorted, shook its pungent, musky fur, and edged away.

In a single, fluid movement, she grabbed the coarse ruff and leaped onto its back. The animal bucked and spun in circles. It brayed in a strange, bawling manner.

"Come on," she called. "Or stay behind."

Trace hesitated. His face flicked through conflicting emotions. Impani leaned low and reached for him. All at once, he jumped behind her. His hands went around her waist.

The beast thrashed and kicked. Its heavy feet stirred a cloud of sand. Suddenly, it ran.

She clung to the scruff of its neck. Flying sand struck her face. She leaned forward, trying to see everything.

The day brightened and painted the sand gold. Shadows fell from a pyramid of rocks. In a valley ahead, several groups of animals stood around a stretch of packed sand.

She sat up and pointed. "Look!"

At that, the beast reared. It bucked and spun. Impani and Trace flew into the air.

She flailed her arms and struck the ground. Pain exploded with the brilliance of stars. She turned her face from the hot sand and gulped the dusty air.

The beast ran on. Its pounding hooves became distant.

Trace rushed to her side. He helped her to sit, his eyes anxious. Then his gaze hardened. "Some tour."

Laughter bubbled in her throat. She got to her feet. "Look what we've found."

Animals clustered in the valley. Some resembled small camels, others bushy goats. They milled about, nervous and skittish.

A lizard creature circled them. It looked like a miniature dragon. It ran on its hind legs, thick tail out, front claws close to its chest.

A predator. If the creature charged them, their closest refuge was the pile of rocks thirty meters away. With a shushing sound, Impani dropped to a crouch and pulled Trace down beside her.

Their bovine friend joined a group of similar beasts. A second reptile slithered about. She expected the herd to run, but they moved only a short distance. As if they waited for something.

Suddenly, the sand rolled. It formed a ribbon that darkened and oozed. The animals stepped toward its edge.

Fluid welled out of the ground. A thick, colorless liquid that rolled in currents like a river. The animals drank side-by-side, even the dragon-like predators. Water dripped in strands from their jaws and left slimy patches on their forelegs.

With a tug at Trace's elbow, Impani crept down the sandy slope. She'd never seen anything so wondrous.

Leaves formed along the river's edge. Green shoots twisted and reached for the light. Then the fluid ebbed. It sank into the ground, leaving a dark strip of depressed sand. In its wake, hundreds of plants shot up. Their leaves unfurled rapidly and spread like a carpet.

The predators moved back, apparently sated. But the other animals grazed feverishly, as if time were running out. Indeed, many of the plants on the outermost reaches were turning black. The heat of the sand was crisping them.

She had to get a sample before they were gone. She pulled out a specimen container.

Trace grabbed her arm.

Fifteen meters away, a reptilian face lifted from a dune of sand. It watched them. Impani's breath caught in her throat. The creature climbed to the top of the bank. It thrust out its neck and opened its jaws, exposing a double row of hooked teeth.

In a low voice, Trace said, "Keep your eyes on him. I'm reaching for my gun."

Impani cringed. Images swam to her mind—the slaughtered beast in the carotene forest, Davrileo Mas smiling. With an inarticulate cry, she leaped to her feet and waved her arms. "Hey, get away from us, you dumb lizard."

The creature blinked then ran straight at them.

Impani spun and headed for the pyramid of rocks. Trace sprinted alongside. His stat-gun was still holstered. He glanced at Impani then looked away, and she felt as if he'd slapped her, called her a fool.

Indignation quickened her pace. Sand kicked up and tapped her back as her stride lengthened. Her boots skimmed the ground. Her belt slapped her hips.

The reptile closed fast on agile legs. Its tail swished the air, sounding like a rapier. It was right behind her.

Impani fled blindly. The rocks loomed ahead. She concentrated on them, memorizing every ledge, every possible handhold. Her vision bounced and blurred with her steps. Her belt drummed against her hips. A stitch spread along her ribcage and ignited an inferno in her chest. The belt dropped off.

The belt!

She dove into the sand.

Trace dodged. "Come on!"

Impani glanced behind her. The lizard leaped and tumbled over her shoulders as if it had misjudged her sudden movement. It landed on its back and clawed the air

She skittered away on her backside. The creature hissed and thrashed. Unable to gain its feet. Trace had reached shelter. She draped the belt about her neck and ran after him.

The mound of rocks loomed above her. Shadow hid the crevices. Where were the handholds she'd noticed before?

She leaped, trying to climb. Her fingers fumbled. Frantic, she leaped again. Behind her, the lizard gave a sibilant snarl. Its tail whipped the air. It was coming.

Where were the handholds?

Impani tore at the unyielding rock. A cry escaped her throat. Suddenly, Trace reached down. She grasped his hand in both of hers and pulled her spent body higher. Her shoulders burned. Her legs shook.

The reptile's claws scrabbled against the rock. Its heavy tail lashed the sand. Impani drew her boots out of reach and leaned into Trace Hanson's arms.

She shuddered, her face screwed up. She could have died, could have gotten them both killed. The dragon creature paced, trying to get at them.

"Why didn't you shoot it?" she asked.

"We aren't here to butcher the locals."

Impani chuckled, wanting only to sink deeper into the embrace of this boy she barely knew. "I think I've had enough sightseeing for one day."

"Come on," he said. "Let's climb to the top of these rocks. Just to look around."

With a reluctant nod, she followed her partner. Wind had scoured the boulders smooth and filled the gaps between them with sand. She concentrated on the climb, flushed with exertion.

At last, she pulled herself to the top. Dunes spread in an endless sea. Regret crested over her. "You were right. We could have walked for hours and not found anything."

"We found the sunken river." Trace shrugged and took the belt from around her shoulders. "The clasp is loose."

"I noticed that when I was dressing. I should have requested a replacement."

"Yes, you should have."

She glanced up at his sharp words, but his expression belied his tone. Trace moved close and wrapped the belt about her waist. Impani held her breath. She felt the strength of his arms about her, felt her flesh tingle with his touch.

What was she doing? He was a criminal, a grim reminder of her past. She brushed his hands away, fastened the belt, and gave it a firm tug.

"I guess we should have searched the caves after all," she said. "Now, we're trapped up here."

"It doesn't matter. Don't you feel it? The ring is coming."

Impani looked at him. Yes, she could feel it—a swirling darkness poised at the edge of her awareness. Emotions warred within. "Drel," she whispered. "It's too soon."

🪐 🪐 🪐

Newton Ambri-Cutt sat behind his console in the control room at the academy. What was Impani doing at that moment? Whatever it was, it was sure to be impressive. She was the brightest cadet he'd ever met. He loved talking to her about his job, seeing that little light of comprehension behind her eyes. It made him proud of her, as if she were his own daughter.

His true daughter, Miriette, was Impani's age. He hadn't seen her in five years, not since the divorce. It was easy to imagine that she and Impani were alike—brilliant and ambitious, a little rebellious. And beautiful. Miriette must certainly be as beautiful as Impani.

A red light drew his attention. As he reached for it, he caught his reflection in the monitor. A bit of gray, a bit more of a paunch, but not so very old. Maybe he should get away from work more often. Socialize. He could remarry. Maybe have another child, a daughter to make him proud.

He could even name her Impani. He would watch her grow to become all the things he'd failed to be, taking Impellics a step further. She would take the academic world by storm; maybe even introduce her old man to computational linguists and script authors as she topped the ranks of computer science.

Suddenly, a klaxon sounded. Ambri-Cutt snapped forward. His console blazed with flashing lights.

Chief Astrut burst into the room. "Holy seas, Newton. What are you doing? Daydreaming?"

"The ring is losing integrity." Ambri-Cutt's fingers flew over the control board, touching lights in sequence, trying to hold the Impellic field together.

"Drel! It's fragmenting." The Chief consulted a panel on the wall. "Override it! We've got people out there."

Impani! Ambri-Cutt gasped. Impani's out there! Sweat ran down his temple. He slammed the keyboard as if he could re-weave the fraying energy by sheer force.

Behind him, the Chief tapped commands into the computer. "Switching to back up."

But Ambri-Cutt knew failure was imminent. With growing horror, he watched the lights turn steady red. His mind raced his fingers, diverting power from one coil to the next, but he was unable to affect the cascading collapse.

Impani.

What had he done?

"My God." He glanced up. "I've lost her."

🪐 🪐 🪐

"The ring can't be coming," Impani said. "They're recalling us too soon."

"Maybe a shortened session is part of the test." Trace walked to the edge of the rock.

She gazed at the dune desert. Disappointment closed over her like a shroud. The ring was coming. Why would they take her so soon? They hadn't given her a chance.

It was over. She should close her mask. At least *look* professional.

Vertigo wrenched her thoughts. She staggered and clutched her stomach as if she'd suffered a physical blow. "Something's wrong."

Trace turned. He reached for her in slow motion. His face elongated.

Impani screamed. She felt the ring twist, felt tearing pain as if her body were turning inside out. Panic stirred a whirlwind in her mind.

What was going on? What was wrong with the ring?

Pulsebeat ravaged her ears. Pressure built until she thought her head would explode. Then darkness grabbed hold, a demon tightening its fist, and she fell into the void.

Chapter 4

Pain. Coldness. Impani turned onto her side. Something scuffed her cheek. The back of her neck throbbed. She groaned and massaged her knotted muscles. She needed sleep. Just a little nap. She would report to Ms. Kline then go straight to her room.

Alarm cut through her dulled senses. Her eyes flew open. She had not returned to the Impellic Chamber. Where was she?

Beside her, Trace sprawled on his back.

She leaned over him and shook his shoulders. "Wake up. Please."

He rubbed his forehead. "You okay?"

She kept her eyes upon his. "No."

With a grunt, he lurched to his feet then drew her beside him. She leaned against his chest and stared at her boots. She didn't want to look. At last, she lifted her gaze.

They stood upon a precipice of white stone, cold and as still as death. Similar columns rose to the horizon–great, craggy monoliths clouded by floating dust. The air had a metallic taint, almost like blood.

"What's happened to us?" she whispered.

He frowned. "I don't know."

She felt an upsurge of panic. "But we're not in danger. Right? I mean, we're only cadets."

Trace lifted the tri-views to his eyes. "Take a reading, please."

"Take a reading? Is that the best you can do?"

"We will not deviate from procedure."

She wanted to punch him. "Who cares about procedure? We have to get home."

He spun about, towering over her. "And when we do go back, I want to be able to say I kept my head. I didn't panic like some coddled socialite disobeying daddy."

Coddled? Socialite? A thousand retorts filled her head. She stared into his hawk-like eyes. "I am not panicking."

"Fine. Then take a reading." He strode several paces away. Bits of flaked stone scattered from his step.

Impani glowered. How dare he suggest she wasn't brave? She was a senior cadet. She'd been at the academy months longer than he'd been.

Why wasn't he afraid, anyway?

Without warning, the precipice jerked. She fell to her knees. A harsh, grating sound reverberated in her chest and tore at her throat. She pressed her hands against her ears and twisted to look behind them at the other monoliths.

The tower next to theirs quaked. Fissures spread like a dark disease. Plumes of dust shot into the air as its surface buckled and dropped.

Impani clenched her teeth against a scream. Rock shards careened about. The thundering air pummeled her like fists then faded into an echoing rumble.

Half the column had fallen. An updraft swirled dust into streamers.

A shudder wracked her body. Could that happen to them? "What if they don't know where we are?"

"Of course they do," he snapped. His eyes shifted from hers, and he knelt beside her. "I'm sorry. I don't know what's going on either. But we have to keep sharp. Most likely, this is part of the training session, testing to see how we react under pressure."

Of course. That made sense. She forced a smile. "Pressure is right. I thought my brain would burst with that last jump."

"Yeah, it was a rough ride." He held out his hand. "Come with me. I want to show you something."

She allowed him to pull her to her feet. Her legs shook as if the column of stone still trembled.

He handed her his tri-views and led her away from the demolished rock. "What do you see?"

Impani lifted the weighty instrument. She adjusted the stereoptics with her thumb. The enhanced image cut through the distance and left the rock stark and bare. She saw column after column, some whole, some jagged like broken teeth. And between them– "Bridges?"

"That's what I thought. There must be intelligent life somewhere."

"We should try to find them."

Trace attached the tri-views to his belt. "Now, you're sounding like a Scout." He walked away across the sweep of stone.

Chagrin filled her. She wished she hadn't voiced her fear that the technicians had lost their lock on them. He must think she was a little kid.

"Be spectacular," she whispered. A moment later, she followed.

The surface of the pillar was cracked, weathered, and covered in rock chips. She sealed a bit of gravel in a specimen container. "It's dusty here. I wonder if it ever rains on this world."

"What's this?" He brandished a slender, whip-like rod at least five meters long. Similar pieces lay at his feet.

She lifted one. "Feels like bone. Flexible. Like the wing of a bird. Look at the different sizes. Imagine a gigantic bird that sheds its wings as it grows."

"That would be unlikely." He tossed the rod away. "Look at these boulders. They're like statues."

"Strange." She circled a pair of lumpy rocks. One sported a weathered face. "Maybe they're tokens. Religious relics. Too bad we can't take a holo."

"I'll save it in my tri-views."

Why hadn't she thought of that? Tri-view field glasses both enhanced and recorded whatever the cadet saw through them. She posed next to a boulder, holding the rod like a walking stick.

Trace skipped backward with the glasses to his eyes, twisting the controls as if unable to get both her and the boulders in focus. He was backing into a pile of fist-sized rocks. She was going to warn him—but didn't.

He tripped and landed hard on his butt. A puff of dust rose behind him.

Impani laughed, but a loud squawk swallowed the sound. She looked around as the two boulders came alive and spread their wings.

❧ ❧ ❧

Trace gaped at the gargantuan birds. They were a cross between pterodactyls and gargoyles. Long, pointed beaks showed rocklike teeth. Their talons were like stone daggers. Their wings had claws at the upper joints, ready to grasp and rend.

Trace scrambled backward. He scattered the pile of rocks as he tried to gain his feet. The great birds took to the air and hovered above him. A huge beak snapped at his head.

Impani swung at them with a whip-like bone. The creatures screeched. They dipped and rose out of her reach as they pecked in turn at Trace. Their wings stirred a whirlwind that peppered him with debris.

A huge talon slashed down. Trace rolled to the side, picked up a smooth, fist-sized stone, and chucked it as hard as he could. The bird caught it in its beak. It had a distensible pouch similar to a pelican. He picked up another stone.

"Don't!" Impani yelled. "Those are eggs."

He glanced from the stone in his hand to those around his feet. He'd stumbled into their nest. That explained why they were attacking him and not her.

Bright, blue light streaked between the birds. She had fired a warning shot. It blinded him for a moment, and he missed being skewered by mere centimeters.

She fired again. This time it was a direct hit. Blue aura encased one of the birds. It squawked and flew higher. Its beady eye turned to Impani.

Trace felt a sudden flare of rage. "Oh, no you don't. You want this?" He hurled the egg. "Take it!"

The bird snatched the egg out of the air. Its pouch expanded.

He pitched the eggs in all directions. The birds darted about with their beaks open, catching them. When he'd thrown the last one, he turned to rocks. He pelted the enormous creatures. "Go on! Get out of here!"

With their beaks full, the birds flew away.

"Good riddance." Trace threw a final rock.

Impani grasped his arm. "Are you hurt?"

He glanced at her, his face hot. "No. Are you?"

She shook her head.

He watched the birds disappear into the hazy sky. His hands shook with spent rage. He didn't know why he got so furious. But when that bird looked like it was going to dive at Impani...

"We'd better get off this tower," he muttered. "They might come back."

"I'm open to suggestions."

"Those bridges must lead somewhere." He headed toward the cliff.

♆ ♆ ♆

Impani holstered her stat-gun. Her heart raced. Those birds might have shredded Trace. And when her weapon had no impact...

She should have warned him to watch where he was stepping but, drel, she didn't know it was a nest.

They stepped along the edge of the precipice. Crevices scarred the rock face. Long-bodied insects darted about their feet. She searched for more boulder statues that might turn into animals. She didn't want to be taken unawares again.

Would it have been possible to ride the birds off the monolith? Either bird had been large enough to carry the two of them. She should have snared one with a grappling hook and lashed herself to its back. That would have been extraordinary.

She filed the idea in her missed-opportunities trash bin and focused on the present. Cold air rasped her face and left a gritty, metallic taste at the back of her tongue. The environmental sensors on her sleeve showed marginal atmosphere.

How foolish—both of them without their masks in place. She'd better not mention that in Debrief.

"I've found a bridge," Trace called.

She hurried toward him. Over the side, she saw two fibrous ropes with a drape of fabric between them. Metal pinions secured the rope to the rock. She touched the cloth, and it rippled like water.

"What sort of people could have woven something so wondrous?" She gathered the slick fabric, and it slipped between her fingers.

He motioned toward the next column. "A hundred meters away, maybe one-fifty. I would like to have seen how they constructed this."

"Maybe they rode birds."

He glanced skyward as if alarmed.

Impani looked at the misty chasm below. Swallowing a flutter of fear, she stepped onto the bridge.

The ropes closed and pinned her body between them. She struggled to step back. The bridge swayed as it released its hold.

Trace muttered, "Now, what?"

"You give up pretty easily for a Scout."

"Whoever made these bridges were either smaller or lighter than we are. We can't get across."

"Well, we can't stand here and wait for the techs to send a ring. The birds might return, or the pinnacle might crumble beneath our feet. Besides, maybe the whole point of this session is to see if we can solve the riddle."

"This isn't a game."

She pursed her lips and turned away. No, not a game. A competition. One she needed to win at all costs. If she was too heavy for the bridge, she would either have to walk on top of the ropes or–

"Wait a minute," she said. "Do you see how the mist rises?"

"So?"

"There's an updraft. I noticed it when the tower fell."

"Impani, I fail to–"

"Hang gliders." She picked up a wing bone and held it in the air. "We can make gliders out of bones and fabric and sail to the surface."

His face remained impassive. "It might work."

"Of course, it will work." Why couldn't he just agree with her? "Look, you gather as many bones as you can. All sizes. I'll slice off a section of cloth."

"All right, we'll try it. But I want you to gather the bone. The bridge may be unsafe."

"I can handle it." She thrust the bone into

his hands and crawled onto the bridge. The ropes closed above her head, encasing her in dusty fabric.

❧ ❧ ❧

Trace watched Impani disappear into the fabric tube. He swallowed a knot of anger. Why was she so difficult? Couldn't she see he was thinking of her?

He swished the wing bone. How did she expect to make a hang glider out of bits of fabric and pieces of bone? He didn't like her idea, didn't like her tone, but most of all he didn't like the way she made him feel about himself. He always believed his greatest strength was his ability to adapt, to improvise.

Why hadn't he thought of a glider?

Impani was a lump rolling inside the bridge. Somersaulting most likely. She managed to move a good fifteen meters from the pillar. A knife flashed as it pierced the fabric and sliced from rope to rope. She gathered the material as she scooted laboriously back to the cliff.

It would have been easier to attach lines to the cut edge and drag it back, but he didn't tell her so.

He retraced his steps to the bird's nest and the cache of wing bones he'd stumbled upon before. With a sense of being forced against his will, he filled his arms. Some bones were so long they dragged behind him and made it difficult to walk. He scuffed his boots and hunched forward for balance. Dust rose with his footsteps.

Suddenly, the surface heaved beneath his feet. Crevices raced across the monolith. He windmilled his arms, throwing off his load.

The pillar was falling. *Impani.*

Trace ran. Rock exploded and shot skyward in geysers of debris. Thunder echoed in his chest. He leaped across spreading fissures, skidding on broken stone. The surface bucked and threw him to his knees. Ahead, the bridge swayed and tugged at the tower. He sprinted toward it, teeth bared, arms over his head against the fall of rock shards.

As he reached the cliff, one of the pinions pulled free. With agonizing slowness, the support ropes parted. Impani scrabbled at the cloth. Her face was pale and stricken, her mouth wide. She lifted her gaze to him.

He felt an electrifying jolt. Textbook scenarios raced through his mind. The bridge shook and dropped another meter. Rock crumbled about its mooring and exposed the final pinion.

Impani climbed the fabric, one hand stretched toward the remaining rope. The bridge flapped as if to shake her off.

He extracted a length of metallic line from his belt and swung it over his head. "Catch!" he shouted as he released the line and sent the barbed end flying. It struck the bridge too high, too far out of her reach.

This can't be happening.

He reeled in the line. With a steadying breath, he threw again.

The metallic line flew outward. She reached for it. But the tower jerked and tossed him onto his back. The line fell short.

"No!" He scrambled to his knees.

Impani lost her grip on the rope. She clawed the slick material as she slid down the length.

He rushed to the rocky cliff, snagged the bridge, and pulled it in by fistfuls. In the back of his mind, reality shifted. A sense of duality stirred.

The Impellic ring was approaching.

Elation filled him. "Hold on! The ring's coming. They're bringing us back."

The frayed edge of fabric ripped. Impani shrieked. She clung to the cloth as it dropped several meters.

What if she fell? She could be dead before the technicians got them home.

With both hands on the exposed pinion, he eased over the cliff. He had to reach Impani, had to help her hold on. His head swam, and he blinked to clear his vision. Hand-over-hand, he shuffled along the rope.

Behind him, the stone pillar broke with the sound of cracking glass. Rock slid into the chasm. Dust filled the air.

Then the bridge heaved a tremendous snap. The metal pinion twisted. Trace froze, fists locked, as the pinion pulled free and the final rope dropped away.

Chapter 5

Impani felt the pinion snap. Her fingers clutched the fabric. She turned her face away, unable to scream, unable to breathe.

The bridge fell smoothly. Drapes of material fluttered around her as she rode the fabric into the chasm. Panic welled inside, belying a vague sense of disbelief.

She was going to die.

Her fingers lost their hold. She fell free. Wind wailed around her and ripped at her limbs. In the back of her awareness, a misty void took shape. Her thoughts leaped with recognition.

The Impellic ring.

Darkness flooded her vision. Tendrils of energy latched onto her being and dragged her from reality. She thrashed and tumbled. Helpless. Hopeless.

Then there was rock. Impani clawed frantically as she tried to break her fall. The surface shifted. Dust rose in an acrid cloud. It burned her eyes, her nose, her lips.

Salt, she thought with abrupt clarity. She was sliding down a mountain of salt.

Fear mixed with wonder. Where was she?

She dug in with her knees, arms outstretched. Gradually, her body leveled. She sat up. Tears streamed down her face. Salty dust ran into her eyes. Her lungs were on fire, her throat swollen and dry.

What had happened? She'd been clinging to the bridge. The stone pillar was falling, but the pinion held—until her partner climbed onto the rope.

Trace stirred from a drift of powder.

Impani turned on him. "What were you trying to do? Kill us both? If the ring hadn't caught us–" She grimaced.

He got to his knees, eyes wide in his white-coated face. He seemed lost, and she was sorry she had spoken sharply.

"You were in trouble," he murmured. "I wanted to rescue you."

"I didn't need your help."

Dust poured from his shoulders as he stood. "Well, where are we, anyway?"

She turned her back to hide a fresh bout of tears then wiped her face with salt-encrusted fingers. Her cheeks throbbed, abraded by the harsh mountain. After a moment, she removed a flask of water from her belt, rinsed her gloves, then dabbed her eyes.

"Here." She held out the flask. "You should wash your face."

"Go easy on the water. You may need it."

A retort died in her throat. Why did he always make her feel foolish? She took a scant swallow of the cooling liquid then returned the flask to her belt.

As she brushed off, she gave herself a quick VSE to make certain that her suit was undamaged. Visual Surveillance of Extremities was one of the first things she learned after being issued a skinsuit. She never appreciated its importance until then.

With one hand over her eyes, she gazed toward the blade-edged ridge of salt. It looked more like a glacier than a mountain—gray and variegated yellow. The sky was blue, the sun bright overhead. The air was still, but she heard the moan of wind.

"Do you still think this is part of a session?" she said. It sounded cheap and sarcastic even to her own ears.

He stood beside her. "Have you ever heard of a ring malfunctioning?"

"Not in any of the textbooks." But she remembered Mr. Ambri-Cutt warning her about the dangers of a fractured ring and how difficult it was to reweave the energy.

If they were trapped in the wormhole, would they keep jumping indefinitely?

Trace took out his tri-views. "We appear to be in a basin. A passage lies in that direction. Can you tell what's beyond it?"

She shook salt out her sonic resonator and wiped the screen. "Readings are inconclusive. The basin must cup the sound waves, bounce them back to us." She glanced up the steep side of the glacier. "I'd hate to be stuck here if that salt begins to slide."

"Agreed." He walked off.

Impani glared. She wanted to rail at him, to vent her frustration. They were in trouble.

Was he never afraid?

Arms about her chest, she trudged behind her partner. The shifting drifts of powder tried to trip her. She edged toward the center of the basin where the salt was packed smooth.

They couldn't be lost. The technicians must know where they were. This was simply an extra-long training session, a sort of final exam. It was just her luck to have Trace as her partner. Why couldn't she have been paired with Natica–or Davrileo? Anyone but this by-the-book, self-righteous, disturbing–

The salt gave way beneath her step. Impani yelped. She sank to one knee, her foot in a hole.

"Hold on," Trace cried. "I'm coming."

"Stay there. I mean it." All she needed was to have him come to her rescue again.

Powder poured around her boot, sucking it under, drawing it deep. She tried to pull free, but the hole crumbled. Salt enveloped her thigh. She leaned back, and her hand punched through the crust.

"Watch it!" he yelled.

That earned him a glare. At least, he remained near the glacier.

Impani sealed her mask. She lay face down on the basin floor then rolled onto her side. Her foot loosened with the new angle. Slowly turning onto her back, she extracted her leg from the salt. The rim caved in beneath her hips. She sucked in her breath, trying to make herself lighter. With both arms overhead, she rolled toward the glacier. The surface crackled with her shifting weight.

"I've got you." Trace scooped her up.

She shrugged him away and looked back. The crater where she had fallen continued to grow. It ate at the crust of packed salt, reaching inexorably toward them. Soon the entire basin would be impassable.

"We can't stay here." She got to her feet. "Let's keep moving."

She led along the glacier's base until she reached a jagged passage. A steady current of air coursed through–as if the basin were having its breath sucked away. A gale roared on the other side. She exchanged a glance with her partner. Lurching over drifted salt, she entered the pass.

Wind howled and tested her balance. Dust tapped her mask. She groped the glacier wall and forced her way toward the jagged strip of sunlight ahead.

The passage opened onto a ridge that dropped five hundred meters. The gale screamed and threatened to flail the flesh from her bones. Impani leaned against the wall and looked out.

Salt rose in steeples and spires, polished by the high winds and sparkling with the sun. Powdery clouds swirled like snow devils. In the distance, the blue sky deepened to indigo.

"Which way?" Trace shouted.

She looked at him. His mask had darkened with the sunlight. It hid his face. She wondered if he was still unafraid. Without a word, she turned her back to the wind and followed the narrow ridge.

🪐 🪐 🪐

Newton Ambri-Cutt's knees quaked. He entered Director Hammond's office. Her assistant motioned him to a chair then closed the door with a click that sounded like a gunshot. Ambri-Cutt took his seat. His shoulders hunched. From beneath his knotted brow, he glanced about the room.

The Director sat behind a huge granite desk. The sides of the desk looked rough and broken, but the polished top glowed with reflected sunlight. Ambri-Cutt swallowed thickly, hands clenched to the point of pain. When the Director looked at him, he cringed.

Her eyes were the color of her desk, her glare cold. She said, "I understand you were responsible for the ring that went awry. Two cadets are lost."

Ambri-Cutt squeaked, "Yes, Madam Director."

"How long have you been with us, Mr. Ambri-Cutt? How many jumps have you handled only to lose this particular ring?" She stood and walked to a sky-lit window. "Do you know who was in that ring?"

Impani. Ambri-Cutt closed his eyes.

"The son of a man so powerful he has lunch with the President," the Director said. "The son of a man who could lobby against us and end the expansion program forever. One wonders if that was your plan all along. To throw weight behind the Mankind First activists who protest daily at our doors."

"No!" Ambri-Cutt nearly leaped from his seat. The thought turned his stomach. Mankind First claimed the exploration and colonization of other worlds was perilous. They charged that public funding would be better spent furthering conditions at home. Their shortsighted whining would lead humankind back to the dark ages. "I am not a sympathizer."

"Nonetheless, that is what I will tell the media when they learn of this fiasco."

"But it was an accident. I didn't mean–"

"What does it matter what you meant?" she snapped. "I am trying to protect the Project. The Colonial Expansion Board is under control of the government, and the government must answer to its people. The public ignores our successes and sees only our failures."

"The CEB will never bow to such pressure."

"They will if the President dictates it. And he's seriously considering spinning us off. A private interest group is offering to take over the program. Private interest. We would be owned. Traded like... a business."

He gawked. "The Board would be dissolved? You can't be serious."

"One more mistake, they told me. One more. Now, you hand me this."

"They don't have to know," he said in a voice he couldn't recognize. "We could stage a rescue."

She barked a laugh. "Those children are trapped in an unstable wormhole. Where in this universe are we to look?"

"Homing beacons. The same beacons that allow the Impellic ring to maintain a lock can be used to pinpoint their location."

"I'd like to meet the person who could accomplish that."

"I can. I know I can."

"Impossible. It's never been attempted." Her gaze flickered. "Besides, they must be dead by now. Materialized upon some gas giant."

"I don't think so." He slid to the edge of his seat. "The rings would still conform to the computer's parameters. They will only drop to worlds with oxygen and water."

She sank behind her desk and winced as if her thoughts were painful. "If they're alive, we can't abandon them."

"I will pinpoint their location, and then you can send two more Scouts—"

"And the new ring can latch onto all four. But is a ring powerful enough to carry that many people?"

He shook his head. "Impellic theorists agree they must jump in pairs. Otherwise, the ring would overload, become off-balanced. No, the rescue party will give them the equipment they need to construct a stronger beacon. Repair the fractured ring."

"What? We're talking about children. They aren't capable of understanding tech."

Impani understands. Impani is brilliant.

But he couldn't tell Director Hammond that— not without causing a new set of problems. Techs like him weren't allowed to be friendly with students.

The Director frowned. Her eyes flicked back and forth as if reading the headlines of a distasteful news report–or her own resignation. After several moments, her cold, gray gaze met his. "You understand that if this plan fails I will use it to further confirm your duplicity."

"I won't fail."

"I hope not, Mr. Ambri-Cutt. For both our sakes, I sincerely hope not."

Impani inched along the ridge. The sandpaper wind roared and lashed her body. She knew she was on the verge of collapse. The constant shush of windblown salt against her mask deafened her. It made her feel closed in, setting her nerves on edge. She couldn't imagine a worse planet to be sent to, couldn't understand why this world would be on the academy's list at all.

A gust struck, and her breath shortened. Her legs faltered, and she nearly fell.

Trace touched his mask to hers. "Just a little farther," he yelled. "There might be shelter ahead."

He'd said those words so many times they no longer had a bolstering effect. Impani didn't know how long they'd walked. Hours may have passed, but the sun never moved. The planet was static—it had a day side and a night side.

He nudged her shoulder to urge her forward. The ledge narrowed and curved. When it doubled back, for a hope-sick moment, she thought it might lead to respite.

But the bend opened onto a whirlwind. Her feet left the ground. The wind slammed her airborne body against the wall and sent her tumbling. She exhaled loudly as she struck the ledge. She couldn't call out, couldn't stop herself from rolling. Another gust picked her up, and she sailed over the edge.

Trace caught her arm. For a moment, she felt like a kite. Wind whipped her and tried to tear her from his grasp. Then he pulled her in.

She lay flat on her back. "I can't do this. I can't keep on." She knew it wasn't the Scout thing to say, knew he would probably report her, but she didn't care. Something was wrong. There was nothing to gain by sending them to this hostile world.

He tugged at her. "Let's go."

"No! I'll blow away again."

"I see a cave ahead. Come on. You can make it. I know you can."

With a groan, Impani pushed to her feet.

She couldn't see a cave, couldn't see anything through blowing grit and dust. It was a ploy. A trick to get her moving again. She'd tell him off if she had breath to spare.

But she followed and found he was right. His cave was more like a cranny. The wedge-shaped crack was six meters deep and wide enough to let them sit. The wind cut as they pressed inside.

Impani fell to her knees. She felt battered. A mass of bruises. Lifting her head, she followed the crevice up the glacier. Blue sky showed above. Silt and dust sifted through sunlight.

"So, what do you think?" he asked.

"I'm tired and hungry."

"I mean about the planet. What's with the salt?"

She sat with her back to the wall and knees to her chest. "We're on the bottom of an ocean. A dried up, desiccated ocean. This world suffered a cataclysmic event. Maybe a comet hit. Or an asteroid. It shifted the axis so it doesn't spin anymore."

"Sounds like you've given it a lot of thought."

"I don't see why we're here. This planet might have been a candidate for exploration once, but it isn't now."

"Maybe they don't know what happened."

"Oceans don't boil away overnight. They had to know. It's like the place was stricken from the viable worlds list, but the ring brought us here anyway. An old computer reference."

"A mistake," he said.

She shuddered.

A shadow passed. It happened so quickly, she couldn't tell if something had blotted out the sky or ran across the crevice mouth.

Trace leaped up. He leaned into the swirling dust and looked both ways. "Wait here. I want to check something."

"I'll go with you." She moved to stand.

He pushed her down again. "I'm heavier than you. I won't blow away." Bowing to the thrust of the wind, he stepped from the cleft.

"Wait!" she called. Where was he going? How could he leave her?

On hands and knees, Impani peered from her shelter. The slanting salt diminished his form to shadow. She leaned farther, staring past her partner to the ridge beyond.

She saw a silhouette. Someone else followed the curving ledge. The figure struggled, weaving in and out of blowing dust. It wore a tight-fitting garment that blended with the color of the glacier.

"Skinsuit," she whispered then realized it was true. They had found one of their own.

Chapter 6

Impani left the cleft in the salt face to lurch against the gale. Her fingers groped the polished wall. A gust struck like a blow to her stomach and nearly knocked her off her feet. She hunkered low, ducking her head and shuffling her boots as she moved.

Perhaps leaving her shelter was a bad idea. She saw no sign of her partner, no evidence of another Scout. If anything, the scouring salt storm was worse than before. She should go back. But she continued.

The glaciers moaned. Salt hissed at her mask. Impani flattened against the wall. Was she going the wrong way? Had she missed a turn she should have taken? She should have caught up with Trace by now.

A jagged crevice winked at her through swirling dust. She staggered toward it, each step countered by rising force as the whirlwind sought to toss her aside. Arms stretched before her, she stumbled blindly. At last, she pushed into a cave.

Trace stood inside. He turned as she entered but did not seem to see her. His mask was up, and his face was raw. A thin line of blood sketched his cracked lips.

"Trace?" she lifted her own mask. "I saw another Scout."

"Gone," he said. "Never here."

The flatness of his voice alarmed her. She moved from the cave mouth to stand opposite him across the swirling floor. The wind sighed and rushed skyward as if caught in a chimney. Outside, it screamed.

She said, "What do we do now?"

He held out his hands. "I followed him. I thought he was real. I thought he went into this cave. But when I got here—"

"A ring must have taken him. They're looking for us."

"We're lost. We're never going home."

"Don't talk like that."

"I can't stay on this stinking world. I've got to get out of here." He rushed toward the entrance across the center of the cave.

"Stop!" she yelled.

The crust of salt broke. Trace sank to his knees. His face darkened beneath its dusty coat. Bellowing, he kicked and stomped—and the salt poured in, drawing him deeper.

"Hold still!"

He seemed not to hear her. He pulverized the floor with his fists. A crater developed about his waist, the salt rolling. A terrified dawning swept his expression. "It's sucking me under!"

Impani dove flat on her stomach. The surface crumbled beneath her. "Take my hand."

"I can't." He gasped. Powder poured around his chest.

"Yes, you can." She strained, reaching. Reaching. Her fingertips latched onto his. "Now, swim."

He closed his eyes, wheezing raggedly. At first, she thought he hadn't understood. Then the crust beyond the crater buckled. He leaned forward and flattened his body as if he were escaping quicksand.

"That's right." She grasped his hand in both of hers.

He groaned and coughed. Silt scattered with his breath. His back elongated and lifted from the salt. Impani grabbed his wrist and pulled.

Suddenly her stomach twisted. The void swirled.

The Impellic ring was approaching.

"Not now," she pleaded. She had to pull him to safety first. He might suffocate before the wormhole took them away.

Darkness ate her vision. His glove slipped from her grasp.

"Hold on." She leaped for his arm. "Got you."

Extreme velocity enveloped her. *Dear Gods of Utopia. Mother of the Seven Hells.* She would pray to anyone if they made it stop, if they led her home. But they were not traveling back to the Impellic Chamber at the academy. They were hurdling to a different world, jumping out of control.

With a wrenching sensation, she emerged into silence. Her ears rang with the cessation of sound. She glanced around.

Green light. Green smell. She lay face down on a tree branch wider than a walkway.

Trace let out a wail. His weight twisted as

he kicked his feet. Impani held onto him, both hands locked about his arm. Her eyes streamed, hot with salt—and part of her marveled at that. How had she brought over a substance from another world? Did the techs know such a thing was possible?

Dust sifted from her shoulders as she grasped her partner's elbow. With all her strength, she pulled him upward.

He climbed onto the branch. "I almost fell. Were you trying to kill me?"

"I was saving you."

"Next time, let me handle things." He sputtered and spat salt. "I don't need help from a girl."

"Fine." Let him handle things? No problem. She never wanted him as a partner, anyway.

She slipped off her gloves, shook them clean, then used them to brush her skinsuit. Her neck ached, and her arms felt torn from their sockets. She pursed her lips. They felt chapped, encrusted in salt. She reached for the water flask, but hesitated and left it on her belt.

The tree limb they stood upon was several meters thick. The bark was dark and shaggy. It gave the impression of extreme age. Light filtered through a mosaic of leaves and turned the air bright green. Branches spread in all directions but with too much space between them to climb. Her gaze followed the limbs overhead.

Movement. Something green. She shaded her eyes. A vine dropped upon her. It wrapped about her forearm so quickly she didn't have a chance to react. It yanked. Painfully. Her feet left the branch.

A scream bubbled up her throat. "Help me!"

Trace leaped to his feet and stared at Impani. She dangled by one arm two meters in the air. He almost laughed—but his attention darted away. Movement flicked along the tree limbs. Snatches of green too quick to be realized.

He frowned and gazed upward. "Is something in the tree?"

"I'm in the tree," she yelled. "Get me down!"

"Stop kicking." He grabbed her legs.

"I can't pull loose." She gasped and struggled. "My arm is on fire."

He gazed up the endless vine. Pale filaments covered its surface—feather-soft hair glistening with moisture, nudging his memory.

She fell limp.

He shook her. "Wake up."

"Trace, please... help me." Her words slurred.

Drawing his stat-gun, he sent an arc of ice-blue energy slicing across the vine. At the same time, an echoing shriek filled the air.

A bird? Just what he needed.

Impani dropped into his arms. He lowered her to the branch and uncoiled the severed vine from her forearm. Slimy residue marred her skinsuit. Her hand was bone-white where the fibers touched bare skin. He tossed the vine a few meters away. It writhed like the tail of a lizard.

His partner's face was pale. Labored breathing. Her emerald eyes were wide. Vulnerable and afraid.

He fumbled to unhitch the med-pac from his belt. "That vine reminds me of the plants we had back home. They grew, oh, about knee-high. We had to clear the fields of them before we could seed." He sorted through the pac and removed the derma-jecter, laying in a dose of antihistamine before snapping the tube shut. He pressed the 'jecter beneath Impani's jaw and felt a pop as it released. "They'd leave runners in the undergrowth, like long, hairy tongues. If anything touched them, they'd coil around them superfast and exude a kind of sedative. When their prey stopped struggling, the plants just reeled them in."

She winced and rubbed the knot that formed from the injection. "They were carnivorous?"

"My father lost his foot to one. I was just a kid, but I was there and that made me responsible." He forced a smile. "Are you feeling better?"

She nodded and slowly sat up. "I guess you saved my life."

He reached for her gloves lying upon the bark. "Let's make a pact. Neither of us will remove our gloves until we return home."

"Deal." Impani examined her withered hand.

He looked away. "I'm… sorry about what I said. You did save me on the salt world."

"I was afraid the salt would crush you."

"At the time, so was I."

"Trace," she said, "it's okay to be afraid."

104

"Afraid?" He scowled. "I'm not afraid."

"I only meant—"

"This is your fault, anyway."

"My fault?"

"Did it occur to you that had we gone to the cave as expected instead of galloping half way across the desert on the back of some beast, the Impellic ring would not have lost its lock on us?"

"That's ridiculous. The ring should have found us no matter where we were."

"Well, it didn't," he muttered.

"I'm not listening to this." She got to her feet.

"Where are you going?"

"Away. Where I won't be a burden."

He leaped up to follow, but stopped. "Go ahead. See what other trouble you can find."

Newton Ambri-Cutt buried his fists in his hair. His eyes teared. "My calculations were correct. We should have found them."

"Maybe they *were* on the planet." Chief Astrut sat on the desk. "But unless you drop the rescue party right in their laps—"

"They may have jumped again. I'll start over."

"They're lost. There is no way to pinpoint them with accuracy."

"But we can get close. And if I can determine the probable area—"

"Go home," the Chief said. "You haven't slept. You've barely eaten."

"If I can calculate their whereabouts, then the rescue party should be able to target them using the same method." Ambri-Cutt slid back his chair. "We need a handheld device, something that will guide the rescuers to the cadets once they're on the planet."

"I don't know, Newton."

"It will work. It has to work." He covered his face. "I can't let her die."

"What do you mean *her?* There are two of them. Why are you so focused on this girl?"

"She reminds me of someone. My daughter."

"Miriette?" The Chief sighed and rested a hand on his shoulder. "She'd be about the same age now, wouldn't she?"

"I always thought I would be there for her. Give her advice about dating. On choosing a career. Now, she won't even accept my messages."

"What do you expect? She's on another world."

"I have no idea what her mother is telling her. It's been five years. You'd think she'd change. Forgive."

"She hasn't changed because you haven't changed," the Chief said. "Look at you. Still putting work first."

"It was the money. There was never enough."

"Is that a ploy for a raise?"

His lips twitched. "I wouldn't turn it down."

"Would you take a vacation then? Maybe visit your daughter?"

"It's too late for that." Ambri-Cutt rubbed his stinging eyes. "But it isn't too late for Impani. I can find her. I know I can. Give me a chance."

"A handheld device, you say? Why didn't I think of that?" He moved toward the door. "All right. I'll speak to the Director."

⊘ ⊘ ⊘

Impani stormed down the mammoth tree limb. Fibers muffled her footsteps. "My fault? How could it be my fault?" She swung her arms, wanting to punch something. "How anyone could stand that unyielding, unforgiving—"

A knoll snagged her boot. She kicked it hard and stepped up her pace. The branch edged to the left. They should be working together. They should be trying to learn what happened to the ring instead of finding fault and pointing blame.

"And to think I let him save my life!"

A rustling sound stopped her. Impani glanced about feeling suddenly alone. Ms. Kline's words came to mind—*scouting is a dangerous business, that's why all Scouts are dispatched in pairs. You have to work with other people.* Of course, Ms. Kline never partnered with Trace Hanson.

"You're a senior cadet," she whispered. "On a normal drop, you would be investigating that sound." *But this isn't a normal drop*, an inner voice answered. "It's probably just blowing leaves." Although she didn't feel a breeze.

She pushed her attention back to the Impellic ring. Malfunctions weren't covered in class, but she'd learned a bit by speaking with

Mr. Ambri-Cutt. Rings were used in sequence. If the sequencer were poorly calibrated, the rings would not align. That would be operator error. Sometimes a ring would fracture under stress, and the operator would have to re-weave the energy or make a substitution. Or on long drops, a ring might dissipate altogether.

She frowned. Each of those scenarios depended upon a tech to bring them home. They would have done that by now. Something must be preventing them from gaining a clear lock. If that were true, perhaps she could correct the problem on her end.

A flower bud nearly a meter in height blocked the branch ahead. Impani edged sideways so as not to touch the filaments at the stem. Her mind remained on the puzzle of the ring. If only she had someone knowledgeable to talk to. If only Trace Hanson wasn't such a stunkard's ass. What was he saying about the plant life of his home world?

The branch overhead rustled.

Impani paused. "Hello?" She gazed upward. All she needed was another vine to drop on her. She had to get out of the tree. She'd feel safer with both feet on the ground.

But where was the ground? She flipped open the resonator and tried to take a reading, but the sonic waves ricocheted off the branches below. All she saw was green haze and crooked shadow. She checked her equipment belt. Grappling hooks and metallic twine would be helpful if she were going up but difficult to retrieve while climbing down.

With a sigh, Impani looked again at the branches above. Their undersides were marred with egg-shaped nodules. Cordlike moss hung in strands. If she could gather enough of that moss, she could make a decent rope. She would loop the moss over the limb, lower herself to the next branch, and then pull it down after. Tedious but workable.

She squirmed on her stomach to the edge of the tree limb and peered at layers of crisscrossed branches. The only way to reach the moss beneath the limb was to climb over the side.

She rummaged through her pouch of hooks and clamps and took out the bear claw. With her fingers linked in the tines, she lowered over the curve of the branch. The hooks bit into the thick bark and drew moisture from the flesh beneath. A screech rose from the shadows. Impani shifted to glance over her shoulder. One of the hooks slipped and gouged a chunk of bark. The screech rose again. Her neck prickled beneath her skinsuit.

She slammed a hook into the surface and moved another meter downward. Muscles burned as her shoulders took on her weight. Mossy cords draped the underside. Rope for the taking—if she could reach it. There were also pod-like growths ranging from centimeters wide to the size of her fist. They resembled the flower bud that had blocked her path. Why hadn't she paid closer attention?

She forced the hooks in at an angle. Her arms shook with effort. Breath burst from her chest. She hadn't paid attention because Trace had annoyed her. It was his fault. Impani snickered then stopped.

The branch at her head rustled. There came a sound. Moist. Sucking. Long, green fingers extended from the branch. They attached to the bark with transparent cups.

Fear welled in her stomach, and she chided herself for it. She was a cadet, trained in first-contact situations.

But instead of introducing herself, she edged back.

A face appeared. Green and lined with veins. No eyes. No sensing apparatus at all, yet the creature detected every gouge, every gash left by her hooks and vomited a thick, gelatinous liquid into them. Its throat pulsed and gurgled as it worked. Its puckered mouth opened without benefit of a jaw.

She moved farther away. Her hook knocked a pod loose. It dropped into the shadows. Moisture dripped from the wound. The creature oozed forward. Its body hugged the branch as if it were part of the tree. The suction of its finger pads crackled.

Impani's shoulders burned. Her fingers ached, locked in the tines of the hooks. Still she edged back. She couldn't explain why, but she sensed that the creature would kill without hesitation or remorse. It was the Guardian of the tree.

It reached the missing pod. Moisture trickled like blood. With its head back, it emitted a keening wail. Flashes of green filled the branches above. Impani cringed. The creature turned its eyeless face toward her. With a rustling sound, it darted forward.

She jerked back. One hook ripped free, and the remaining hook tore a long gash in the tree. Another creature appeared. Then another. Impani leaped for the drape of moss. She wrapped her fingers around the cord and dragged it with her as she fell. The tree became a blur.

She hit the next branch and rolled with the impact. The length of moss remained attached to the bark above. Creatures swarmed about the limb. They dropped from the higher branches.

With a tight grip on the moss rope, Impani swung to the next branch. The cord tore from the tree, and she hit the branch hard. She scrambled to her feet and bolted down the broad tree limb, coiling the moss as she ran. The limb forked, and she followed it to the right. A large flower bud blocked her way. She crouched behind it. Panting, she listened to soft thuds as creatures dropped to her level.

Suddenly, the flower bud shuddered. Cracks split the sides. The fissures quaked as if something inside were pounding to get out. The top peeled back, exposing an interior of cottony white fibers.

Green fingers punched through. Then an eyeless face. The creature squirmed and strained to extract itself. Fibers draped its shoulders like wet cobwebs.

Impani gaped. She couldn't move, could not force herself to look away. Then a bolt of blue-white energy arced overhead. It struck the branch and nearly knocked her over the edge.

"This way!" Trace yelled over the resulting shrieks of the creatures. He stood on the opposite fork, waving his gun.

Impani wasn't sure if she was angry with him for being there or with herself for feeling relieved that he was there. With the coil of moss over her shoulder, she leaped. He caught her before she plowed over the other side.

"They're like antibodies." He fired again at the blackened limb. Bark flew as if exploding. "That ought to keep them busy for a while."

The branch lurched beneath their feet. As one, the eyeless faces turned toward them.

"Or not," Trace said.

Her head swam with her footing. "Is this tree sentient?"

"It's certainly aware of itself. And of us."

The creatures grouped together. They seeped along the bark. Trace took a step backward. With his gun, he motioned to the branches above. The tree was filled with green organisms. Hundreds of them.

Impani's heart pounded in her throat. "If the tree is intelligent, we might be able to communicate, to explain that we mean no harm." Immediately, she pictured her hooks ripping the bark. She looked down at the scorch marks left by Trace's gun.

"Run," he said. "I'll hold them off."

She opened her mouth to disagree. They were not there to butcher the locals, and whether the tree was sentient or not, it was just trying to defend itself. But a sudden shriek pierced her ears. A creature swooped at them as if from midair. Trace fired. It exploded with the same force as the bark.

"Run!" he yelled.

And Impani ran. Trace continued to shoot. She didn't look back. She felt sick. This was a slaughter. How could fright overrun her values so easily? Then a creature struck her shoulder, and she clubbed it away with her fists.

Darkness crowded her vision. Her stomach wrenched. The ring was coming. The void swirled to claim her. She knew she was running, could feel her arms and legs pump, but the tree limbs were gone. Nausea burned the back of her throat.

Then agony hit as if it were a physical barrier. She flattened against it. Her body elongated. Stretching. Ripping. Her eyes bulged until she thought they would burst, but she was powerless to close them.

Somewhere she heard a scream, terrified and pitiful, rising in pitch. Part of her mind took census, a mental patting of her pockets to find her passkey, and she realized she wasn't the one who was screaming.

It was Trace.

Chapter 7

Impani appeared on a new planet, materializing a meter above ground and falling with a thud. She rolled onto her back, dazed, and looked up at a bright orange sky. For a moment, she imagined she could still hear the keening wails of the tree organisms. Then she realized the sounds were real.

She leaped to her feet.

Trace thrashed on the ground, covered in green creatures. She rushed to pull one from his face. Her fingers sank into its mushy flesh.

He heaved a deep breath then yelled, "Get them off me! Get them off me!"

She reached for another. Its body popped like a pustule, coating her gloves in viscous slime.

"They're dead," she told him. "Liquefying."

He sat quickly. "My eyes. They spat at me."

"Can you see?"

"Ugh. They burn."

"Let me wash your face."

She knelt beside him, dampened her fingers from her flask, and wiped his eyes. His skin was blotchy. Deep lines marred the creases of his lids.

"Let's make a pact," she said. "Neither of us will remove our masks for the duration of this trip."

"Deal." He winced and looked down at the green sludge in his lap. "What a mess."

"Apparently, they can't live without their tree."

"But how could I have brought them with me? They're from another world."

"I have a souvenir, too." Impani held out her moss rope. "This must be why the techs make us take a decon shower after every session."

"We'll have to be careful. We don't want to contaminate an alien eco-system." He patted his belt then located his gun lying beside him. "Where are we this time?"

"We're on an island." She motioned at smooth, green water. Other brown nubs marred the calm surface—almost like stepping-stones. "There are more."

Trace took out the tri-views. "Must be thirty or forty, all small like this one, just a few meters wide."

She tested a sample of water. "This ocean is thick with microorganisms. Primordial soup."

He looked at her, eyes wide, then locked his mask in place. She did the same.

"I wonder why there are no plants." She scrubbed at the bald lump then scooped up a handful of dust. "Doesn't feel like normal dirt."

He rapped. "Doesn't sound like it, either."

Abruptly, the island lurched. Impani cried out and sprawled on her back. The island lifted and propelled forward. Water creased before it as it picked up speed.

Peering over the edge, she saw wide flippers. "We're on an animal, a turtle of some kind. We must have startled it."

"Not us." His gaze moved upward.

Impani looked up as enormous, saw-toothed jaws snapped down. She shrieked and rolled. The creature resembled a dinosaur: huge head, tiny eyes. Triangular teeth chomped at her as if she were a tantalizing morsel.

Trace yelled, "Jump!" He dove into the water.

She stared after him in surprise and dismay. The massive face bore down on her yet again. With a muffled cry, she crawled toward the edge. But the turtle jerked and tossed her back. Her faceplate slammed its shell.

The turtle rose high on the water's surface and began to spin. Impani slid on her stomach. She heard a roar, felt a jarring impact. Then she flew into the air and splashed into the water.

Green darkness closed over her head. The filters of her mask popped. Through the thick water, she saw the outline of a huge leg. Battling a churning undertow, she angled for the surface.

The once tranquil ocean fell to chaos. The turtle creature continued to spin, turning the sharp edge of its shell into a blade, while the predator snapped and roared. Impani back treaded and looked for Trace.

A grating squeal made her cringe. The predator caught the whirling shell in its jaws. Blood sprayed in fat drops. The turtle stuck out a horned head, and then another.

Two heads. She stared, fascinated.

Trace grabbed her shoulder. "They're diving."

Turtle islands all around were sinking into the ocean, taking with them any chance of escape. If she didn't catch one while it was still upon the surface, she'd be left treading water.

"Come on!" She swam hard, pacing one of the creatures.

It was large and gnarled. Heavy flippers stroked smoothly, unhurried.

Probably too old to panic.

She latched on, hoisted herself on top, and then glanced to see that Trace had followed. Slithering forward, she looked for the turtle's heads.

Only one was visible. The neck extended and recoiled as the creature swam. Timing the movement, she lowered a loop of moss rope into the water and caught the lunging head. She pulled as if with reins. The turtle bucked.

Roxanne Smolen

"What are you doing?" Trace asked.

"I'm trying to keep it from diving. Help me."

He took one end of the rope. They yanked and hauled to keep the creature's head up. It swam faster. Flippers broke the water like oars. The other head poked out. It elongated and retracted as it worked in tandem with its counterpart.

Impani reared back to keep the rope taut. They left the other turtles behind. The predator disappeared. Perhaps its appetite was sated.

"Land ho!" Trace pointed. "Let's see if we can steer in that direction."

A mist-shrouded island came into view. She pulled with all her might. At last, the ponderous head turned. They approached a sandy shoreline dotted with purplish scrub.

"What do you think?" she said. "Real dirt?"

"Looks real." He leaped from the animal as it beached itself. "We were lucky the turtles were there."

"What do you mean, lucky? I was almost an appetizer."

"Without them, we would have materialized in the middle of an ocean."

Another bad computer reference. The ring was following outdated programming. Impani loosened the moss rope. She coiled it around her hand and elbow then slid down the shell.

The turtle looked larger out of the water. Its flippers were motionless upon the sand. Both heads were out. The neck that took the brunt of the reins looked red and abraded.

"It's exhausted," she said.

Trace knelt beside a purple bush and plucked a small white melon. He tossed it toward the turtle. "Hungry?"

"Don't," she said. "What if it's poisonous?"

"Then it won't eat it."

But the turtle did eat. It crunched loudly. Impani grinned. She picked an armload of the pale fruit and rolled them across the sand. The creature ate with both heads, beaks snapping at each other as it rooted for more.

"It likes them." She joined her partner.

He gave her a rare smile.

With a roar and a torrent of water, the predator rose from the ocean. It opened its jagged mouth and bellowed. The monster's oversized head made it look like a T-rex. But as it stood, muscular forelegs emerged, exposing huge, webbed claws.

The turtle churned the sand, unable to attain its defensive spin. Rex lumbered forward. Dark green water roiled about its knees. It bent low over its helpless prey.

Trace drew his gun and fired. Energy bolts crackled over the beast and leeched into the water. Rex roared and staggered. Vapor steamed from its body. Teeth bared, it turned toward Impani and Trace.

Impani pulled her weapon. They fired together. The blast threw Rex backward with a tremendous splash. Waves crashed onto the beach. Its mighty tail lashed the surf as the beast swam away.

The two-headed turtle edged toward the water. Its flippers gouged the sand. Moments later, it disappeared into the ocean.

Impani's hands trembled as she fumbled with her holster. She no longer felt confident in her stat-gun. It hadn't worked against the gargoyle birds. And if she and Trace hadn't fired at the same time, it might not have worked against Rex. She didn't want to kill anything. That wasn't why they were there. But what if it was necessary? What if she had no choice?

What if she had been alone?

Scouting was dangerous business. That's why Scouts were sent in pairs. She didn't have to be friends with Trace to be a good partner. But it would help.

"That was an adventure." She smiled. When Trace didn't comment, she added, "At least, you're no longer covered in green goop."

"The sun is setting. I don't want to walk around a strange planet at night."

She looked up. The bright orange sky had faded to rust. "When we get back, we should complain. Our masks should have infrared or night vision."

He shook his head. "That would make them too heavy. Let's find someplace to rest."

They walked into the deepening brush. Mist and shadow obscured their path. Impani felt like she was walking upon a cloud. There were no trees—but a vast variety of bushes snagged her knees. Pale melon shone among the foliage.

"I wonder if we should gather some of the fruit," she said, "now that we know it isn't poisonous."

"We can't eat on an alien world. Real Scouts go three days without food. They have pellets."

"We don't. That's another thing we should complain about."

He picked up a melon and sliced it in half with his knife. The core was blood red, the flesh striated with purple veins. Maggot-like worms squirmed and fell.

He tossed it away. "I'm not hungry enough to eat that."

She gulped. "Me neither."

In single file, they trudged away from the ocean. The grade steepened. Before long, they edged along a narrow path that zigzagged up a cliff. Three moons lit the night, and the mist glowed eerily.

"Feel that?" he said. "The rock is vibrating."

She pressed her hand against the wall and felt a tremble. "It's rhythmic. Like it's breathing."

"Maybe we should go back down."

"To where?"

He shrugged and continued to climb. The path grew slick. Moisture streaked Impani's mask. The growing vibrations rumbled in her chest and made her fear they were climbing toward a sleeping giant.

When they reached the top of the cliff, they were enveloped in steam and the roar of geysers.

"We're on the rim of a volcano," Trace shouted. "I bet the island was formed by an underwater vent."

"What now?"

"Are there any caves?"

"Plenty." She showed him her resonator.

He frowned at the screen. "Let's go here. The entrance is obscured by a geyser. It might be safer."

"Wait. You want to climb into a volcano?"

"We need to rest." Without a backward glance, he picked his way through gushing water.

A ball of fear constricted her throat. She peered into the volcano's black maw. Fingers of mist laced the depths. Something fluttered. Bats. Dozens of them.

If they can do it, I can.

She followed her partner over the rocky surface. Geysers rose and fell. The taint of sulfur seeped through her mask. "Stop. We're right above it."

He knelt. "Distance?"

"Fifteen meters straight down. I can't make that climb."

"Sure you can. I'll sink a bolt anchor here, and we'll use your rope to rappel down. All right?"

She sighed. "All right."

Apprehension clenched her stomach as she watched him secure the bolt.

"You go first," he said. "Yell when you get there."

She took a flashlight from her belt and clipped it to her wrist. Then she knotted the rope around her waist.

"See you in a minute," he said.

She nodded numbly and lowered over the edge. The wall was like black glass. She kicked off and moved down several meters. The geyser struck like a battering ram. Breath left her in a painful *oof.* She clung to the moss rope as water shunted her to the side. Out of control, she dropped another meter.

The water receded and left her spinning. She struggled to gain her bearings. Her shoulder slammed the crater wall. She closed her eyes.

"Almost there," she whispered then continued down.

She'd planned to shine her light into the cave before entering in case it was the lair of some beast. But the geyser roared again. Water threw her into the cavern. She landed awkwardly on one hip, her light bouncing over the rock. Several bats fluttered around her head. Up close, they looked like striped kittens with wings. When the cave mouth cleared of water, they flapped outside.

Impani untied the rope. She tugged it twice and called, "I'm down." The rope reeled in.

With her light aimed before her, she explored the cave. It was small and irregular, perhaps seven meters at its widest point. In places, the ceiling barely cleared her head. As she walked, she heard a steady drip of water. But then the geyser roared again, and she lost the sound.

Without warning, Trace burst through the steaming curtain and sailed feet first into the cave. He landed as neatly as a gymnast. Impani scowled. Her hip still stung from her fall.

He said, "Here's your rope back. Are we alone in here?"

"It appears so." She accepted the coiled rope and draped it over her shoulder. "I was investigating the sound of water." She trained her lamp into the depths of the cave. The geyser ebbed, and she could again hear the musical drip.

The ceiling slanted downward, forcing her to crouch as she followed the sound. At the farthest reaches of the cave, she found a meter-wide basin worn into the floor. It brimmed with liquid.

Her mouth went even drier at the sight. Fumbling through her supplies, she took out her kit and tested the water. "It's good," she said in a husky whisper. "We can drink this."

Trace dropped to his knees. He slid his mask to the top of his head and splashed his face. "That's better."

Impani cupped her hands beneath the persistent trickle then scrubbed the remaining salt from her eyes and nose. She removed her flask from her belt, drank it down, filled it from the basin, and drank again. It tasted vaguely sweet. Her empty stomach swelled. Refilling her flask, she sat beside Trace.

"Real Scouts carry a canteen that replenishes itself from humidity," she said. "Add that to our list of complaints."

"Yeah." He motioned at her wrist lamp. "You should save the batteries."

"Right." She switched it off. In the darkness, the gushing geyser looked bright. "Why do you know so much about nonpoisonous melons and carnivorous vines?"

He gulped some water then pulled his mask in place. "I grew up on Andromeda Four."

"You're a farmer?" But farmers were rich.

"My father's a farmer. I… left."

"How did you end up in a penal colony?"

He leaned away and stared.

Impani shrugged. "Everyone knows."

Silence fell between them, and she thought she'd pushed too far. She leaned against the wall and latched her mask.

He gave a heavy sigh. "I wanted to travel, so I took a job as an off-loader on a freighter.

Boring work, but I hoped to see a lot of worlds. That's what the poster promised, anyway. So on my first night in port, my friends and I were sightseeing. I headed back early. I stumbled across a man assaulting a woman in an alley, and I jumped in to save her. It turned out that the woman was an underage girl and her assailant was a prominent government official. The local authorities needed to hush it up, so they twisted the facts and made it look like I was a vagrant trying to rob him."

"But the girl was a witness."

"She refused to testify. Scared, I guess, or maybe they bought her off. So, I was sentenced to hard labor. Then they found out that I'd lied about my age on my application with the freighter. I was sixteen at the time."

Impani stared at Trace Hanson. She couldn't have been more wrong about him. "So, the judicial system cut a deal with the colonization program?"

"They couldn't leave me in the mines. I was too young. Even so, my father had to call in some favors." He shook his head. "What about you? Where are you from?"

"Nowhere near a farm." She laughed a little too loudly. "I never even saw a tree until the program."

"City girl, eh?"

"Something like that." She looked at her hands. A farmer's son. They weren't alike at all. What would he think if he knew she grew up on the streets—homeless and uneducated? A fiery blush crossed her cheeks.

At least, I was never in a penal colony.

But she had done far worse than rescue a girl in an alley.

"I wonder where we'll jump next," he murmured.

"It isn't where that's important but why. We have to figure out what caused the malfunction. How well do you understand Impellics?"

"Well enough, I guess. But they didn't cover malfunctions in class."

"I have a theory. We know that a drop consists of a sequence of rings. I think the final ring in our session fractured and is wobbling, trying to break free. The instability pulled the other rings out of sync."

"No, it can't be the final ring or it wouldn't keep latching onto us." He massaged his neck. "It must be a middle ring. The last ring picks us up, trying to send us home, but we hit the fractured ring and the wobble spits us out somewhere else."

"That makes sense. So, how do we bypass the middle ring?"

"We don't." He glared as if he doubted her sanity.

"So we just give up?"

He stretched out on the cave floor, hands behind his head. "Wake me at daybreak."

She drew in her knees and hugged her

chest. There had to be a way to stabilize the ring. She watched the flowing geyser and let her mind drift, willing it to land on inspiration. The steamy curtain brightened. She crawled to the cave mouth and gazed outside.

"Good morning," she said.

"The sun's risen already?"

"Short night." A shadow passed over the cave mouth. She skittered backward. "Something's out there."

Trace shot forward and pulled her away as an enormous snakehead parted the rushing water.

Red and gold patterned the snake's pebbly face. Its fangs curved inward, saber-toothed, and a tongue flicked between them.

Impani gaped. Her heart beat so hard, her entire body shuddered. The snake's milky-white eyes turned toward her. Water splashed and pounded its head, sounding like rain on tarp. After a while, it pulled from the cave.

141

Trace looked outside. "It's gone. I guess we didn't smell like food."

"This is drel. I want to go home. We have to figure out how to fix the ring."

"I'm sure the technicians—"

"Forget the technicians. If they could bring us back, they would have done it by now. We have to do this ourselves." She stood to face him, daring him to contradict her.

Then nausea struck. Her stomach wrenched as if a grappling hook were wedged behind her naval.

The ring was coming. She wanted to curl into a ball, wanted to weep, to rail at the injustice. She couldn't keep doing this, couldn't stop doing it. There was no help, no end.

The Impellic ring pounced. It ripped her away from reality and twisted her gut until she thought she would faint. She smashed against the barrier and tore her way through, falling. Falling.

She landed face down in the dirt. With a whimper, she curled onto her side. A tear splashed her mask.

Trace shook her. "Do you smell that? Forest fire."

"I don't smell anything."

"We're upwind. It's coming this way. What's the terrain like?"

Groggily, she took out the resonator. "Trees. Hills and gullies. A river in that direction, but it's pretty far."

"Let's go."

Favoring her bruised hip, she climbed to her feet. "Are you sure there's a fire?"

He took off through the forest, calling over his shoulder. "Hurry. We can't stay here."

Impani looked at a soot-gray sky. The trees were tall and thin, the branches fanned like the tail of a bird. They whipped about as if the forest itself was attempting to flee—but the air where she stood was stagnant and dry.

143

With a sniffle, she hugged her arms. Her gaze fell upon the coiled moss rope in the dirt. She snapped it up, draped it over her shoulder, and hurried to catch her partner.

He stood at the top of a steep rise.

Embarrassed by her outburst, she smiled as she joined him. "How can you smell a fire if your mask is latched?" She'd meant it as a teasing reference to the pact they'd made about not taking off their masks. But he looked at her with an almost painful seriousness.

"That bothers me, too. These masks aren't airtight. Think about it. We're only supposed to jump to class m worlds. The filters neutralize any unfriendly gases we encounter, but…"

"We can still suffocate in a fire." She nodded. "Let's keep moving."

Boots skidding, she led down the slope. Tufts of yellowed grass tangled her ankles. As they crested another hill, she caught a whiff of smoke.

He took out the tri-views. "Nothing but trees. Can you find a clearing?"

"In that direction." She motioned with the resonator.

Bounding from trunk to trunk, they followed an animal run down the slope. A gully ate the base of the hill. It was black with muck. She leaped to drier land. Trace stared at her.

"At the top of the next rise," she said to what she thought was his question.

"Hear it?" He turned his back on any answer and climbed quickly away.

She was about to shout *hear what* when a distant roar reached her. Fire. She glanced upward. A flock of birds passed overhead, wings beating.

Fear gathered in her throat. She followed the root-strewn path up the hill, grasping trees for support. Puffs of dry soil kicked up with her footsteps. Her boots felt like lead.

Keep moving. But she was hungry. Tired.

Her muscles burned with each step. By the time she reached the top, she was panting.

Trace stood in the clearing. He pivoted on his heel as he peered through the tri-views. "We're closed in. We have to find shelter. Locate a cave or something."

"What cave? There's nothing here."

"We can't outrun it."

She snatched the glasses from his hands and looked out upon the trees. Smoke billowed and churned. She saw a glint of water. "The river. If we're quick, we might make it."

He looked to where she pointed. Then he frowned, head tilted. "What was that?"

"Come on." She headed across the clearing.

He went the other way.

Fear and anger raced through her. "The fire is coming."

She could hear it clearly now—the thrum of a thousand drums. Panic gripped her, rooting her with indecision. Finally, she followed her partner as he pushed through the trees.

The ground was uneven, making her footing treacherous. She slammed against tree trunks, sliding and dislodging loose stones. Ahead, Trace crouched low and melted into the prickly brush.

She ducked beside him. "What's going on?"

He motioned toward an animal caught in a stand of sapling trees. Wisps of smoke rose from its fur. "We can't leave it."

"All right." She huffed out a breath. "We'll free it and go. We're nearly out of time."

🪐 🪐 🪐

Trace looked at the large animal. Its hindquarters were heavy but the forelegs were finely drawn, as if the beast stood upright. The front hooves were splayed almost like fingers.

147

Hands outstretched, he approached the creature through the trees. "There now, my friend. You can't stay here."

The animal raised its head, eyes wide in pale fur. Its muzzle was snubbed, its mouth upturned as if in a smile.

"Gently, gently. What seems to be the trouble?" He moved in a slow circle, wide of its reach.

The creature's hind leg had caught in the young trees. Bone splintered through the skin with the weight of its thrashing. The saplings were supple—the beast would never break loose.

He bent over the fractured leg. How could he free it without causing more damage? Sweat fogged his faceplate. He lifted his mask so he could see.

Immediately, his eyes watered. He coughed into his glove.

Impani moved behind him. "Look."

Flames encroached upon the hill. It glowed as if it wore a halo.

"No time." He removed his gun.

"What are you doing?"

"What do you think?"

"Can't we just free it?"

"Take a good look." He pointed. "The thing's a biped. It can't run on one leg."

She knelt to stroke the animal. He glanced back at the glowing hill. A hot wind rose.

"You can't kill it." She stood between them, arms folded. "That's not why we're here."

"I can't let it burn to death, either."

He pushed past her toward the creature's head. Its eyes, black and piercing, bore into his.

"I'm sorry, my friend," he said, "but you're too big to carry. This is the best I can do."

Its stare held his. He raised the gun.

Please, a voice not his own said clearly in his mind.

149

Chapter 8

Trace jumped back. Had the animal spoken?

"Trace," Impani said.

"Did you hear that?" he asked her.

"I hear the fire. We have to go."

He shook his head. He'd heard it say please. Please kill it? Please don't? Either way, he couldn't murder an intelligent being. "Give me your rope. And go cut a few branches. We have to make a litter."

Her glare sharpened. She hurried away.

He snapped the mossy rope between his hands, testing its strength. Ash pelted his face.

With fingers over his mouth and nose, he appraised the broken leg. The ground around it was scuffed black.

Pain said the creature.

Some sort of telepathy. Trace knelt beside it and stroked the pale fur. "Don't worry, buddy. We'll get you out of here."

He glanced toward Impani as she scored the base of a long branch with the beam of her stat-gun. On the hill beyond her, the aura grew.

He jammed his boot in the crook of the trap and spread the saplings. The creature moaned and writhed. It pulled its mangled leg free. Bright red blood smeared the bark.

"How much longer?" he called over his shoulder. Hot cinders rained down. He covered his face with his arm then locked his mask.

"Here." She carried over eight poles roughly two meters in length and charred on each end.

With a nod, Trace wove the poles together with the rope.

⬭ ⬭ ⬭

Impani watched her partner's fingers as he deftly knotted the rope about the wood. She looked at the animal. Its eyes were closed, but its chest rose with long, regular breaths. Patches of burned fur showed pink, blistered flesh.

They were going to die trying to save this beast. She glanced at the sky. The lowering smoke was tinted orange with the approaching blaze.

Trace tossed a piece of wood toward her. "Strip the bark off this one."

"What are you making?"

"A sled. I hope."

She bit back a scathing reply. Taking out her utility knife, she slashed the surface of the pole. The bark peeled back like paper. The wood beneath was smooth and slick. As she worked, an acrid stench seeped through the filters of her mask. Heat leeched through her skinsuit.

The forest fire had found them. Flames lapped the surrounding brush and ran the length of the tall thin trunks. Trees cracked with the sound of breaking bones and crashed to the ground, showering the air with sparks. She covered her head and stifled a scream.

"Help me with this," Trace called over the sound of burning.

She hesitated. Reflections of flame danced over his mask—with her among them. Swallowing a catch in her chest, she knelt at his side. They bowed the pole she'd stripped of bark and affixed it as a single runner to the bottom of his sled. Then they wedged the platform against the creature's back and lifted it, balancing the heavy beast on top.

"Take off your belt," she called. "We have to strap it down."

Coughing, Trace held out his belt.

She tried to connect the belts together, but her buckle wouldn't hold. Panic rose to her throat.

He yelled, "We've got no time."

Hands shaking, Impani forced his belt to latch onto hers. She tossed the length over the creature's chest and secured it to the poles. "Let's go."

Holding opposite sides of the platform, they rocked the makeshift sled. The runner creaked and dug deeper into the dirt.

"It's too heavy," she yelled.

Fire claimed the trees at the edges of her vision. Her head swam with smoke, and she imagined her skin searing to the inside of her suit.

The sled moved—slowly at first, and then faster. The creature stirred, but remained silent. Steadying the platform, they steered it down the hill.

She struggled with her grip on the sled, fought for balance on the skittering rocks. As the roar of the flames receded, the haze grew. Trees shot as if from nowhere, striking her shoulders as she thudded through them.

The creature's face was rigid, eyes squeezed shut. Its body jounced, and its heavy rear threatened to spill onto the ground, but the belts held.

The ground leveled. The sled slowed.

She panted. "Now what?"

Trace stumbled and glanced about. "I didn't plan past getting down the hill."

Impani pressed her lips tight against mounting anger. What did he mean he had no plan? He was going to get them killed. They should have freed the beast and let it take its chances–just like them.

She heard a crash and a crackle as fire circled the far side of the rise. They would never outrun it. They needed to find shelter.

But the smoke was too thick to see her resonator screen. All she recalled of the area was a hill carved with animal runs and a gully of... Muck. Wet, rotten leaves.

She twisted the platform about. "This way."

They forced their burden over the dry ground. Dead brush sprouted from dust to tangle the runner.

Impani licked sweat from her upper lip. Her legs trembled against the sled's load. Through heavy haze, she made out the gully. Trace seemed to guess her strategy and redoubled his efforts. They manhandled the sled toward the dark mire.

The ditch was eight to ten meters long, less than two meters wide. She reached in and could not feel the bottom.

"It's wet." She shook her arm. "But no standing water."

"Get the belts off," Trace said. "We'll dump him in easy and run for the river."

Impani unhooked the belts from the sled, but the clasps had tangled in the long fur and she couldn't remove them from the animal. "They're stuck," she cried, ripping at the buckle.

"Let's get him in first," Trace said.

The sled tilted, and the creature made a startled sound as it fought the slide.

"There, now," Trace told it. "Just leave the work to us."

He cradled the leg as the heavy body fell into the mud. Blood streaked his skinsuit. Crawling into the trench, he scooped armfuls of black leaves onto the animal's fair pelt. Muck reached over his knees.

"It's not deep enough," he said. "He's too exposed. We'll have to tilt the sled on top."

Impani looked back at the approaching flames. Brush hissed and crackled. "What about the belts?"

But Trace was already dragging the platform. She hurried to help him. They pulled the sled until it formed a lean-to against higher ground. The wood cleared the muddy creature by scant centimeters.

"Coat the top." Trace scooped handfuls of muck onto the poles.

She climbed into the ditch. Mud sucked at her boots. With a rotten log, she pushed more sludge toward her partner.

Dark, dripping leaves heaped the overturned sled. The creature looked out with frightened eyes.

"That's good," he yelled. "Let's go. Let's go."

He leaped out of the pit and ran. Fire raced him along the dry brush. A glowing rift appeared in a tree. The trunk split.

"Look out!" she cried.

He slid on his backside, arms over his head. The tree fell as if in slow motion. Flames skimmed the ruptured wood and flew in streamers. The trunk knocked over thinner trees as it bounded toward him.

Impani rushed to her partner. The burning trunk crashed to the ground. A flurry of sparks filled the air.

"Get up!" She beat cinders from his suit.

He raised his head, eyes wide, face gray behind the faceplate. His lips moved, but she couldn't hear what he said.

She shook him. "Get up!" Her skin was crisping.

Heat radiated from the trunk. Flames sprang wherever sparks met the ground. The air turned blue with smoke. On the hill, fire leaped in quickly moving patches. It roared and snapped. Another tree fell.

Her throat constricted. Couldn't breathe. She fought the impulse to strip away her mask. With a strength borne of panic, she dragged him to his feet.

Trace glanced about as if lost. Superheated air rose in waves around him. "Go back." He tugged her toward the gully.

She blinked with distorted afterimages. Her skin felt shrunken and tight. She stumbled after him, clutching her chest and coughing.

He dove headfirst beneath the lean-to. Smoke rose from the ends of the muck-covered poles. Dreamlike, Impani slid into the mud. She crawled beneath the sled and squirmed behind the creature. With a start, she closed her hand over the forgotten utility belts tangled in the animal's fur, and she clung to them as the blaze surrounded the gully.

≋ ≋ ≋

Director Hammond drummed her fingers upon her desk, still staring at the phone's blank screen. She couldn't believe the vote had gone against her. What a political nightmare. The Colonial Expansion Board may have no choice but to disband. After all these years, she was going to be out of a job.

A knock sounded at her door, and Mogley stepped in. He'd probably been watching her on the in-house, waiting for her to disconnect. She didn't like Magnus Mogley. She knew the Board assigned him as her assistant to spy on her department, but that wasn't what bothered her about him. It was his patronizing, ingratiating tone, as if his main role was to keep her quiet until all decisions were made.

"They've got their stay of operations," she told him. "The courts have officially shut down the academy. And do you know how they're doing it? Child labor laws. They claim the Colonial Scouts program exploits teenaged children."

"That's easy enough to avert." His round face beamed as he sat across from her. "Just raise our age requirements to, say, twenty-five."

"Do you know the difference between a fifteen-year-old and a twenty-five-year-old?"

He spread his hands. "Experience?"

"Exactly. And experience equals caution. A fifteen-year-old kid wouldn't hesitate to skate down the walls of an ice hole or parasail over a volcano. They might think it was fun. We wouldn't learn half as much about these alien worlds if our Scouts were of age." She rubbed her forehead. "On the other hand, if they were old enough to have degrees in Impellics and Theory, we might not be faced with the problem we have now."

"That is why I needed to speak with you, ma'am. Chief Astrut reports that his technician has refined his calculations. They're ready for a second rescue attempt."

"We can't," Hammond said, knowing he would report anything to the contrary. "I've been given my orders. No one makes another jump. As of this moment, the Impellic Chambers are off limits." She looked away. Those poor children. Their safety was her responsibility. Now they would die because of political red tape. Even if there was a way to save them, she had no authority to try. "Private ownership is beginning to look better all the time."

🪐 🪐 🪐

Fire raged down the hill like a living entity, consuming everything in its path. Impani clung to the belts. She burrowed deeper into the side of the gully. The pliable mud yielded to the pressure of her back. Trace's arms encircled her shoulders. The animal pressed against her legs. A coppery taste filled her mouth, and she realized she had bitten her cheek.

Something struck the top of the sled, and all three jumped. A flaming branch rolled over the edge. Then a tree fell into the gully, hitting the ground with a loud crash. Sparks flew from the trunk. They struck the lean-to and hissed in the mire.

Impani shielded her head. Screams moved up her throat in fist-sized bubbles. Oh God, oh God. She looked at the burning tree. Tears rolled down her face and spattered the inside of her mask–and part of her shouted *stop it. You'll need the moisture.*

A branch bounded off the platform, knocking it askew. The creature fell limp. She clung to its body in terror.

Then nausea struck.

She recognized it immediately–an Impellic ring was forming to claim her. But instead of relief, she felt growing rage. Why was this happening? Each planet seemed worse than the last. Her stomach twisted as the void spiraled nearer.

Trace turned as if speaking, but she couldn't hear him over the fire, couldn't see his face through the haze. Another tree limb struck.

The rope snapped. With a clatter of poles, their meager shelter fell apart.

Then the ring latched onto her. The flames turned dark. The world receded.

Impani groaned. With one hand, she gripped the creature before her. With the other, she clutched the belts. Trace's arms wrapped her chest so tightly she could barely breathe. She hit the black barrier with a sensation of ripping open and twisting inside out.

Then her butt bounced on the ground. She blinked against sudden bright light.

White sky. White stone. Cold air sifted through the filters of her mask. Tears burned her eyes, and a sob hiccupped in her chest.

"We made it," she whispered.

"No. Oh, no," Trace said. "It's dead."

Only then did she realize the heavy creature still pressed against her legs. Wisps of smoke rose from its fur.

She yelped. "The animal came with us?"

"It was sentient. It spoke to me."

"But that's impossible. Impellic Theory states that a ring can carry only two people. We shouldn't have been able to bring something this large through with us. Tree organisms, maybe, but—"

"The jump must have killed it," he murmured. "Or maybe it lost too much blood. Ah, drel. I wanted it to live. I wanted to save it so that something good would come out of this mess."

Impani grasped the belts still knotted in the fur. As she pulled them free, the broken buckle opened and revealed a line of blinking lights. She cracked the case farther, peering inside. Something tugged at her memory.

She'd seen a similar configuration in the control room with Mr. Ambri-Cutt. "This is a homing device." And the significance of the words crashed over her. The belts let the ring know where they were.

But they hadn't been wearing the belts.

"Trace, this is a homing device. The belts were on the beast. We didn't pull it through the wormhole. It dragged us. If you hadn't been holding onto me…" She gasped. "You would have been lost."

"I thought they just —" His voice choked. He took his belt from her hand. "Let's make a pact. We don't remove our belts."

She looked at the twinkling buckle then closed the case and snapped the belt around her. What else hadn't the instructors told them? Did they think the cadets were too young, too stupid to grasp the concept? Impellic Theory was just that—a supposition about something no one truly understood. If they were old enough to jump to alien worlds, they had the right to full disclosure.

Deep in disgruntled mutterings, she jumped at a jab to her shoulder. A dark being with a shiny exoskeleton glared down at her from the other end of a spear. She nudged her partner. He gasped. Slowly, they rose to their feet.

Three beings stepped from behind the first. Their mouths were beaklike, and they chattered and clicked loudly. Each had four arms that were constantly in motion.

They looked like oversized ants with kilts, which would be funny if not for the spears. She raised her hand. "We come in peace."

The chattering quit. They edged back.

The first ant pulled himself up to his full meter-and-a-half height and said clearly, "Kkind travelers. We thankk you for thiskk offering of meat."

"You speak Standard?" Trace asked.

"I am Kkrick." The ant creature lowered its head. It wore a long, gray scarf to match the colorless kilt. Its chest was decorated with smears of blood. "You mustkk be handlers?"

With a puzzled frown, Impani looked at Trace. His mask had darkened against the bright sunlight, and she saw the reflection of the ant instead of his face. She took a breath to ask Kkrick how he knew their language.

Trace spoke first. "Yes. We are handlers."

"Much kkgood." The insect-like face contorted into a horrific smile.

"How did you find us so quickly?" He motioned to the empty plain.

"Patrollingkk."

"Patrolling against what?" Impani asked.

"Incursion, of course. Other clans are notkk to be allowed across our land. Come. We mustkk feast."

Without looking back, Kkrick strode away. The other three ants surrounded the dead creature. Although it massed more than their combined weight, they picked it up over their heads and trailed after their leader.

"Handlers?" Impani whispered. "What are you thinking?"

"I think we're in trouble." He followed Kkrick.

Impani stifled a laugh that edged toward hysterics. Trouble? They'd been in trouble since the beginning of the session. She was too tired for more adventures. She wanted to go back to the academy, give her report, and sleep for a week.

Pursing her lips, she caught up to her partner. She had to walk quickly to keep up with the ant-beings. Her muscles protested, and the air seeping into her mask was so cold she thought her lungs would freeze. At least, it dispelled the smell of smoke.

"Why are we following them?" she muttered.

"We've been invited to a feast. It would be impolite to refuse. Besides, they have spears."

"They have spears, we have guns."

He chuckled. "Whatever happened to we aren't here to butcher the locals?"

That stopped her. How could she let uncertainty and fear affect her beliefs?

Embarrassed, she said, "I don't like bugs."

"Well, if they're anything like the bugs on my home world, they are strong, warlike, and numerous. And they excrete pheromones. If we kill Kkrick and his friends out here in the open, we'll have a hundred more on us before we can find a place to hide."

Impani looked around at the plain of flat white stone and suppressed a shudder. She didn't want to stay on this world. "Have you noticed that each drop seems a bit longer than the last?"

"You think there's a time limit to our tour?"

"I think we'd better figure out what's wrong with the ring before we're left on a planet permanently."

Trace nodded and fell silent. Impani increased her gait. How could ant creatures outpace her on such spindly legs?

Her thoughts returned to her belt. The buckle contained a homing device, she was certain. The belts must use a beacon to call the ring to their position. If the main ring needed such a device, it followed that each subsequent ring needed the same beacon in order to latch onto them. If they had a stronger beacon, it might jar the errant ring back into alignment. But how did they build a stronger beacon?

Her footing slipped. She caught her balance, suddenly aware that they climbed a slight grade. The flat stones lay upon themselves like carefully placed shingles.

Another squad of ants chattered and waved as they passed. One had a fist-sized spider impaled on the tip of a spear. He held it over a red fissure in the rock. The spider's legs kicked then curled as if touched by extreme heat. It gave her the bizarre image of a campfire and marshmallows.

The rise steepened. Kkrick and his party climbed. They held the dead creature high overhead. Impani's boots skidded. Stones skittered beneath her step. She perspired, although she felt thoroughly chilled. She wished she could sit beside a fissure.

The number of ants around them increased. Many wore kilts, but some were naked. Their smooth exoskeletons shone in the bright sun. They clicked their beaks and ogled them. Kkrick walked without preamble toward a hole in the ground.

She cringed. "We aren't actually going in there."

"Is that a problem?"

"Yes, it's a problem. We'll be trapped."

"I don't see that we have a choice. Besides, we're handlers now. That seemed to hold some sway."

She stared at the hole, sweating harder than ever. "What do you suppose is for supper?"

"I suspect it will be the creature we brought from the other world." He shook his head. "I keep telling myself that dying of smoke inhalation is better than burning to death."

"With any luck, the meat will poison them."

One by one, Kkrick and his followers disappeared into the huge anthill.

Standing on the rim, she peered down into the darkness. "No." She stepped back. "We can't go in there. Too dangerous."

"It might be more dangerous if we don't." Trace motioned at the many ants around them. He placed his hand on her shoulder. "Come on. We're cadets. Don't you want to know how these creatures live? They're fascinating."

"They're bugs."

"We need to eat something."

"You said we couldn't eat on alien worlds."

"On a normal drop. But this isn't normal. And I don't know about you, but I'm starving."

Impani winced. He was right. Until they found their way back to the academy, they would need to keep up their strength.

"Go on down," he coaxed. "I'll be right behind you."

She nodded but wanted to kick herself. From the beginning, she'd hidden her claustrophobia from her instructors. Now it was coming back to bite her.

With fumbling fingers, she located her flashlight and clipped it onto her wrist. Waves of gooseflesh ran up her arms. *I can do this. I'm not trapped. I can leave at any time.* She stepped onto the ridge that surrounded the hole then down into the dark.

The tunnel was narrow and steep, lined floor-to-ceiling with flat stones the size of dinner plates. Red crevices pulsed like veins, making her feel like she was crawling down a monstrous throat.

The ceiling forced her into an uncomfortable crouch. She stretched her arms to the walls, afraid of falling. The pancake-like stones teetered beneath her weight. Her legs shook, and her back ached with strain. The flashlight cast a thin beam into the dark. It only served to accent her terror. The walls closed in as if the tunnel meant to swallow her.

"I can leave at any time," she repeated like a mantra.

Sweat ran down her spine. She concentrated upon placing one foot before the other. How deep was she now? How much deeper would she be forced to go?

Then, when she thought she could stand no more, the tunnel opened. Impani stumbled to a halt, feeling dwarfed and insignificant as she gazed at the vast city of the ants.

Chapter 9

Impani goggled at a cavern at least one hundred meters high. Dimly lit caves honeycombed the walls. Ants popped in and out. They climbed slanted terraces. Light touched their gleaming carapaces and turned their bodies gold.

Several other tunnels emptied into the cave—but only one was flanked by flaming torches. Mist hung before it in low clouds.

"There they are." Trace motioned.

With a sort of fascinated dread, she watched Kkrick's cohorts scale the wall, still carrying the dead beast. They reached the first terrace and disappeared into a cave. Kkrick turned to look at her. She felt his gaze like a stab to her stomach.

Curse Trace for talking her into climbing into this death pit. She was not the least bit interested in how these bugs lived.

Trace prodded her. Woodenly, she walked toward Kkrick. Ants watched with unblinking eyes.

Kkrick bowed. "Do you wishkk to bathe before eatingkk?"

"No, we just... bathed," Trace said.

"Much kkgood. Come to feast. I take you childrenskk way." He walked up a ramp to the first terrace.

The walls were rippled and pocked. Ants scaled the surface as if upon ladders. They seemed anxious to catch a glimpse of the newcomers.

Kkrick led to another terrace and then another. Impani glanced down. Below them, ants poured from the tunnels into the city. There were hundreds of them. Their horrible clicking sounds echoed in the vast space. Again, Trace prodded her.

She continued upward along the slanted ledge. The cave openings she passed were octagonal. Through the filters of her mask, she smelled moldy dirt. And something else. Death. Like the old tombs and crypts in the cemetery where she'd grown up.

Kkrick stopped. He motioned her toward a cave. Impani dug in her heels, and her partner walked into her back. She looked at Trace, pleading with her eyes for him not to force her to go in there.

🪐 🪐 🪐

Trace smiled encouragingly at Impani, although he wasn't sure she could see him in the gloom. He bounced on the balls of his feet, excited to see more of the hive. He remembered the ant farm he'd kept as a boy, remembered watching day-by-day as the ants built their kingdom.

He glanced at the opening of the cave. Like the other caves they'd passed, this one smelled of freshly overturned soil, reminding him of his father's farm. The impression of welcome faded with the impatient clicking of their guide.

"Kkrick wants us to go in," he said to Impani. "That's right, isn't it? We should go inside?"

Kkrick nodded. "Sticky."

Trace ushered Impani through the opening into a round vestibule. The floor was indeed sticky and oddly resilient, as if he walked upon netting. Strands draped down. They adhered to his faceplate when he brushed against them.

He looked up. The ceiling danced with gold-green lights that scuttled over one another. The lights were alive.

"Spiders." He nudged Impani. "Look. They have phosphorescent patterns on their backs."

She didn't reply. Why wasn't she intrigued? What kind of Scout hated bugs?

Kkrick stepped behind them. He plucked a spider from the wall with two prehensile fingers. Holding the wriggling arachnid, he bit into its body. It sounded like he was eating a crisp apple.

He held the spider toward Trace. "Much kkgood."

"No. Thank you." Perhaps he'd been wrong to hope for food from their hosts.

Kkrick shrugged, which was an odd sight on a creature with four arms. Still munching his snack, he led them through another entrance into a larger cave. The room was well lit and warmed by torches blazing from the walls. It looked like a chamber in a medieval castle.

Five ant-beings lounged around a stone table in the center. They wore ill-fitting togas woven of knobby thread, which Trace assumed was spider silk. Their chattering clicks sounded remarkably like laughter. They drank and sloshed about large, metal goblets and took no notice of Impani and Trace.

"Has the feast already started?" Trace asked in a hushed tone

"Always they are here," said Kkrick. "Always eatingkk. They feed the kkqueen."

He swallowed a jab of unease. Who was fed to the queen? He puzzled through Kkrick's words, then said, "They fill their stomachs then regurgitate for her?"

"Unless she hungerskk more and takes them whole." Kkrick laughed at his own joke. "Come. Feast."

He clicked and waved at the group around the table. They stopped their revelry and moved to the end to make room.

Kkrick bowed to Trace. "I tell them you are handlers of the otherskk."

Impani stepped forward. "And who exactly are these—"

Trace squeezed her arm. "Kkrick, where are the others?"

"They come. We choose kkcommanders to feast and pay homage to you."

"And it was through these commanders that you learned to speak our language?"

Kkrick stared. "Of course."

Impani wrenched her arm away. "I'm going to be sick."

"Relax. If there are others here who speak our language, they might be able to help us get home." He guided her to the table.

They sat cross-legged upon the floor. A sour smell filtered into his mask. Probably mead. He grinned and glanced around. A platter held a tangled pile of spiders, apparently roasted, their legs curled over one another. Bones the size of human finger bones littered the stone tabletop.

The other creatures glared as if they'd ruined the party. Their black eyes were large and reflective. Trace shied from their gaze then jumped as Kkrick set down two goblets of green liquid. It looked more like bile than mead.

"I'm not drinking that drel," Impani rasped.

Trace smiled and nodded as if she'd said something complimentary. He held a goblet toward her. "Look at this workmanship."

Impani gave him a blank stare.

"I'm not joking. Such metalwork is thought to be impossible for creatures without opposable thumbs."

"Maybe the others made it for them," she muttered.

Trace scowled. Her attitude was not befitting a Scout. He was just about to tell her so when another creature came into the room.

This one was smaller and had a reddish sheen to its shell-encased body. He carried what appeared to be a water-filled bladder. The newcomer sat on the edge of the table. With the bladder between his knees, he began to knead and stroke it rhythmically. The bloated organ let out an eerie sound, like a sheep's bleat echoing from a deep well.

It took several moments before Trace realized it was music. He glanced about the table. The ant creatures sat with their heads inclined, mesmerized by the throbbing tones. All conversation stopped.

Then a parade of creatures entered, each with a platter of meat. The aroma of a barbeque filled the air. The food bearers set the platters on the table while the bladder musician played on.

Trace's stomach growled. But before he could move, a ruckus came from the entryway.

"Kkgood." Kkrick stirred lethargically. "Otherskk are come."

A man and a woman were shoved into the room. They wore heavy, standard-issue winter clothing. Their faces were pale and gaunt, their eyes ringed with fear. Then their expressions hardened.

"Scouts?" the woman cried hoarsely. "Colonial Scouts?"

She lunged toward Trace and Impani across the table. The man scrambled to catch her, holding her back. Froth flecked her lips, and her reddened eyes bulged.

"Kill you!" she screamed. "I will kill you!"

Natica Galos stared in disbelief at the man behind the podium. The academy was suspending operations? But what about the rescue? What about Impani? She glanced to either side at the other cadets in the assembly hall. They were just sitting there. Wasn't anyone going to speak up? Didn't they see how wrong this was?

She glimpsed Robert Wilde at the back of the room and felt a stab of anger. He pretended to love Impani, but he was like the rest. No one was speaking out for her.

Sinking lower in her chair, Natica turned her gaze back to the Director's Assistant at the head of the room.

※ ※ ※

Robert Wilde was so furious he expected his brains to boil out of the top of his head. They were terminating all sessions, including the rescue. Those stupid, frigging—

He glared around as the other students filed out the hall. They were all politely shocked, all secretly relieved that it hadn't happened to them. None of them gave a drel about Impani.

Wilde closed his eyes, trying to imagine where she might be. There were so many planets within reach of an Impellic ring. Was she safe on a green world or trapped in a nightmare?

God, they've terminated the rescue. No way to know what she was going through. Worse yet, she was out there with Trace Hanson. Wilde imagined Hanson putting moves on Impani, taking advantage of her fear and confusion. He pictured him laughing as if he had her all to himself, stepping up for her kiss—

Wilde leaped to his feet, knocking back his chair. Impani was his girl. She loved *him*.

He glanced about. The room was emptying. At the entrance, Natica Galos stood talking to Mr. Mogley. Wilde stormed ahead, but before he reached the front of the room, Mogley left. He approached Natica. Her face was blotchy. Crying. That only made him angrier.

"Well? What did he say?" Wilde demanded.

She blinked at him. "Robert, I really can't—"

"Did you convince him to keep looking?"

"No."

"Why not?" He grabbed her arm. "Are you just going to let her die? What kind of a friend are you?"

"He said he doesn't have the power."

"Then who does have the power?"

Her eyes widened as if he'd made some revelation. She yanked her arm from his grasp. "Sorry, Robert. I have to go."

Wilde frowned as she rushed from the room.

Chapter 10

Impani leaped up, gawking at the hysterical woman. These people looked like colonists. What was going on?

Kkrick stood. In one fluid movement, he vaulted over the table and shoved the woman backwards. She slammed against the wall then sank to her knees, holding her head with a dazed expression. Impani stepped forward to help her but became suddenly aware of the ants watching as if appraising her reaction. She stood where she was.

The man rushed to the woman's side. "Marie. Are you all right? Can you stand?"

Kkrick grabbed the man by the scruff of his coat and tossed him so that he landed near Trace's feet. He clicked, "Respectkk your handlers."

The man shuffled forward on his knees. "Help us. Please. No one leaves this place."

"What are you talking about?" Trace pulled him to his feet. "Who are you?"

"I am Avid McCleary, hydroponics engineer of Colonization Project Number B1X-39-4A. We came to this planet because the Colonial Scouts said it was uninhabited." He gave a barking laugh, tears flowing. "Uninhabited. They didn't know, didn't take the time."

"Colonists?" Trace asked. "How many?"

The man's face contorted. "They keep us in the paddock. They feed on us. Like cattle."

Impani touched his shoulder. "Mr. McCleary, how long have your people been here?"

"Five years," he said dully.

Impani stepped back. Five years. Five years of terror, of watching those closest to you die, all because a Scout made a mistake. Because of incompetent reporting.

Tears stung her eyes. She slid back her mask and ran a hand over her face.

The room erupted.

"You are not handlers!" Kkrick chattered, pointing at her. "You are otherskk. Like them!"

And Impani realized why they had been treated with deference. Kkrick had mistaken their skinsuits for exoskeletons. He thought they were a new type of ant, probably feared they were on the brink of war for feeding on the colonists without permission. He thought they were in charge—like him.

With a wave of his many hands, Kkrick directed several ants into the room. Each carried a spear. Impani reached for her gun, but they were on her, their bulging, glassy eyes close to her face, spear points at her throat.

Their horrible clicking voices echoed in her ears. They yanked her arms behind her as they propelled her body forward. She glimpsed the other ants at the table still watching. Glimpsed the woman propped against the wall.

Avid McCleary's terrified wail came behind her. "Don't leave us! Don't leave us!"

Impani struggled to look around. All she saw were bobbing spearheads. "Trace?"

"I'm here," he called, his voice strained.

"Can you reach your gun?"

He hesitated. "No."

Her eyes widened. Don't panic, she told herself. Remember your training. But she couldn't recall a classroom lecture that covered man-eating bugs.

She stumbled out onto the terrace, her hands wrenched painfully behind her back. The ants moved faster than she could walk, and they half carried her through the city. Their limbs were twig thin and stiff.

Her flesh crawled. They ate people. Colonists. She pictured the platters of cooked meat, the bones upon the table. What if she and Trace had eaten at that feast?

She gagged and nearly fell. An arm tightened around her waist. She felt herself lifted into the air and carried into a tunnel. Darkness closed around her like a fist. She sensed the ceiling scant centimeters above her face. Her eyelids fluttered, and she must have fainted because the next thing she knew she was being carried feet first up a narrow incline.

Cold air slapped her awake. She struck the ceiling. Dust and pebbles rained into her eyes. Light gleamed upon the ants' heads as they swarmed beneath her. Their wretched two-fingered hands pinned her arms, her legs, as they bore her out of the passage.

Stars twinkled above. Impani gulped fresh air as if she'd been drowning. She lifted her head, trying to see where they were taking her.

Spotlights streamed upward like a halo around the shadowy outlines of Quonset huts. People moved within the light. Colonists. She thought of the woman's reaction to seeing two Scouts after five years on this world.

Suddenly she was propelled through the air, thrown into the compound. She rolled with the impact, pulled her stat-gun from its holster, and pointed it at the ants.

But Trace was already up. "Bugs! I hate bugs!" He fired his weapon, strafing the night with electric-blue discharge.

Impani played her wrist lamp over the empty plain. The ants were gone. What sort of creatures could move so fast? Then she heard voices behind her.

"They're Scouts," someone said. "Come and look. It's not Avid and Marie at all. It's two Scouts."

"Colonial Scouts?" a woman asked.

"Holy seas. It is."

Impani turned to face a dozen colonists. She holstered her gun then spread her hands, trying to think of something to say. But she remembered the despair in Avid McCleary's words. What could she tell these people?

The colonists clustered around them in a semi-circle, their faces stark in the spotlights.

"Come back to admire your handiwork?" snarled a man.

"This is your doing," said another.

"Stop it!" A woman swatted him. "Don't you see? They can send help."

"Is that true?" A man stepped forward. He had a thick scar across his cheek. "Can you get a message out?"

Trace stammered, "W-we're not in contact—"

"But you're Scouts. Someone must have sent you."

"What's all this?" A woman bustled toward them through the streaming light.

"Newcomers," said the snarling man.

"Soldiers brought them."

"They're Scouts, Missus. They're going to help us."

"Is that so?" Missus said.

Impani had the sense that she was being appraised. She decided anything she said would make the situation worse, so she stood in silence at Trace's side, glancing from face to face.

Finally, Missus said, "It will be lights out soon. Get on home, all of you. There will be time enough in the morning to discuss who will help who."

With excited whispers, the crowd disbursed. Missus walked up to Impani and Trace.

"You're not real Scouts, are you?" she asked quietly. "You're children. Here by mistake."

"We're cadets," Trace told her.

"We were in a training session," Impani said. "The Impellic ring malfunctioned."

"I didn't think they'd resend Scouts to such a thriving community." She chuckled without humor. "I'm Cassandra, but they call me Mrs. Fixes. I'm the maintenance mechanic."

"I'm Trace, and this is my partner, Impani."

Missus nodded. "Like I said, it will be lights out soon. Best get you to shelter." She turned and addressed a shadow within the light. "It's all right, kids. They're harmless."

A girl stepped into the open. She carried a young boy, but he wriggled from her grasp and ran toward them.

Missus scooped him up. "My son, Timothy."

Impani's stomach dropped. "There are children here?"

"Timothy's the first to be born on this planet. We were so happy. That was before the soldiers came." With her son in her arms, she headed toward the huts. "I'll put you in a storage shed with a portable heater. It's going to get cold."

Impani couldn't imagine it getting much colder.

Trace said, "We haven't eaten and…"

"Well, food is one thing we have plenty of. Lathi, why don't you bring over some of that leftover stew?"

The girl's face lit, and she ran off. She was barely in her teens. Too young to live with such horror.

Missus yanked open the door of a domed shed and strode inside. She pulled several thick blankets from a shelf. "Sorry I can't offer you a bed. We'll see to better arrangements in the morning."

Would they still be there in the morning? She wanted away from this terrifying world.

Then Lathi came in with two covered dishes.

Trace took the plates from her. "Thanks."

"Lathi, take Timothy and get straight home," Missus said. "I'll be there shortly."

"Yes, ma'am." Lathi took the boy from his mother's arms and rushed out of the dome, letting the door slam.

Missus dragged a battered cylinder from the corner and knelt to toggle a switch. She struck a panel with the heel of her hand, and a light blinked.

Impani felt a rush of warm air. "Is Lathi your daughter?"

"She is now," Missus said. "Soldiers took her parents."

Dread filled Impani's stomach. She moved nearer her partner. Trace handed her a plate and lifted the lid. Steam burst upward. Impani stared at the dark stew.

"Vegetables," Missus said, seeming to read her hesitation. "From the hydroponics lab. I don't know what we're going to do now that Avid is gone." She stood and brushed her knees. "Stay inside. You don't want to be walking around the paddock after lights out. I'll see you in the morning." With a nod, she walked into the night.

"Sounds ominous," Impani said. She'd meant to be flippant and was embarrassed by the quaver in her voice.

Trace stared at her. "Are you all right?"

"Why doesn't the ring come?"

"It will. We'll get out of this."

She bit her lip to keep the fear within her from finding its way out. Replacing the lid, she set the plate on top of the heater. "Did you hear what she said about them not sending Scouts to an established colony?"

"I suppose they think there's no need."

"But don't you think they should? Just to be sure everything's going well?"

"Expensive."

"Not as expensive as human lives. These colonists are right. Scouts are responsible." She looked at him. "But you'd think they'd fight back. They must have weapons."

He spread a blanket before the glowing heater. "Come eat some of this food."

Impani cringed. She sat beside him and stared at her plate. Trace ate as if ravenous. She tried not to watch. With the tip of her tongue, she tasted the stew. The gravy was rich with savory herbs. She bit into an unrecognizable vegetable. Chewing woodenly, she glanced around at the shed.

The metal walls were scuffed and battered as if the hut had been moved several times and hastily put back together. Rows of shelves stood from floor to ceiling, all of them crammed so haphazardly with crates and equipment she wondered how anyone could find anything.

Abruptly, the lights went out. She stiffened and nearly choked on another bite. In the dark, the coldness intensified. The frigid air laced with waves of heat and gave the semblance of a breeze.

"I wonder how long night lasts," Trace said.

The question dug a hollow in her stomach. She set down her plate. "I can't eat."

He drew the edge of the blanket around them. She was aware of the nearness of his body, and found herself trying not to move so he wouldn't lean away.

"I'm sorry," he said quietly. "You told me that climbing down that hole was a bad idea. I should have listened. I could have gotten us killed."

"If we'd refused to follow them, they just would have realized we weren't ants that much sooner."

"What do you think they'll do with us?"

"I don't know," she said. But she knew very well what they were going to do. They were going to roast them until their legs curled and serve them on platters. Why didn't the ring come? She hid her face in her hands.

"Cold? Here, lean against me." Trace slipped his arm around her.

She pressed against his shoulder, but no warmth seeped through his skinsuit. She tried to relax but shivered instead.

"They must be looking for us," he said. "I know my father wouldn't give up. I'm sure your folks won't either."

Impani blushed. She felt like she'd been caught in a lie. What would he think if he knew what she was, where she'd come from?

He said, "You never told me why you hate enclosed spaces."

She pushed away and looked at him.

He smiled. "It's pretty apparent."

"I was a kid," she said, the words out before she could stop them, "and I was looking for food. I got trapped in a trash compactor. The lid snapped shut behind me. I spent the better part of a day and a night in there, darkness pressing down on me, things skittering over my arms. Next morning, they started up the compactor. Luckily, they heard my screams."

Trace chuckled. "Yeah, right."

"I'm not kidding."

"But you said you were from the city."

"City streets. I don't have a home or parents. I was abandoned as a newborn—something I will never understand or forgive. An old woman found me at a bus stop. She said she'd thought I was a kitten. I'd been making mewing sounds. So she named me Impani after a cat she'd once had. We lived in a cardboard carton."

"You were homeless?" Trace frowned.

"Yes, but I didn't feel homeless, you know? It was as if the streets were my home. The old woman looked out for me, taught me right from wrong. Funny. I never knew her real name."

"Where is she now?"

"She died. I was about ten. After the compactor incident, they sent me to an orphanage. I hated it there—so structured, so closed in. But one good thing—they taught me to read. I ran away two years later, but I kept reading everything I could. That's how I found out about the Colonial Scouts."

"Wait. You say you have no formal education. You're totally self-taught. And you made it this far?"

She shrugged. Was he doubting or judging her?

He let out a low whistle. "You are nothing like what I expected."

Impani felt his words crash over her, felt undeniable despair, and she realized that she had wanted him to like her—because she'd started to like him. "Sorry to disappoint you." She turned to conceal her tears.

He caught her chin in his hand and tilted her face toward his. "You don't disappoint me."

Her breath trembled in her throat. She parted her lips, anticipating his kiss. But he hesitated. She looked away. What was she thinking? He was a farmer's son. Rich and powerful. What would he want with a common girl like her?

"We'd better get some sleep," he said, huskily.

She glanced at his shadowed face, wishing she could see his eyes, wishing she knew what he was thinking. He tucked the blankets around them then pulled her close. She laid her head upon his chest and listened to his heartbeat. His breath tickled her cheek.

He'd been about to kiss her. Even knowing she was homeless, that she had no family, no history. Would he be so free with his attentions if he knew the other half of her secret?

His breathing slowed as if he was asleep. The heater's red glow tinted his profile. What if he could love her? What if she finally found someone to trust?

She snuggled against his side, lips still tingling with the almost kiss, thoughts drifting into dreams.

❧ ❧ ❧

A tumultuous crash shook her from sleep. Impani bolted upright, heart pounding, struggling to free herself from the blankets. She heard another loud bang as something large struck the side of the shed.

Trace threw open the door. Sunlight burst inside. Dazzled and confused, Impani stumbled to her feet and stood beside him. She heard shouts and the sound of running. And clicking.

"Bugs." Trace strode into the yard.

Impani leaned out the door. People ran in all directions. An ant scurried over the roof of an adjacent hut.

"What's going on?" Trace shouted as he stepped into the melee.

He grabbed a man who pushed him away and kept running. Trace walked deeper into the yard, waving for attention.

An ant moved up behind him.

"Trace! Look out!" Impani yelled.

The ant wrapped him in its four arms and lifted him neatly overhead. Trace kicked and screamed. Two other ants grabbed his legs.

Impani ran forward. She pulled out her stat-gun and pointed it helplessly. If she shot, she might hit Trace. She held the weapon in both hands, fingers on the trigger as the ants carried her partner from the compound.

Chapter 11

Impani stared as the ants carried Trace away. She saw his face, his eyes upon hers, saw his lips move. Calling her name.

"No!" she screamed.

She fired her stat-gun at the ant pinning Trace's legs, knowing that her partner would feel the jolt as well.

Ice-blue energy enclosed the creature and crackled over its armored body. It fell away as if in a faint and twitched on the ground.

Missus called to her over the cries of the colonists. "Energy weapons won't work. They just shake it off."

To Impani's amazement, the ant climbed to its feet and retook its place beneath Trace.

Impani bared her teeth. She shot the creature again. As it toppled, she ran toward it, resetting her gun as she had when she cut down the branches on the forest-fire planet.

"Shake this off!" Standing over the ant, she fired a narrow beam directly into its eye.

The creature's head exploded, spattering her boots with yellow jelly. She looked up, ready to cut down the next ant—but they were already out of range.

"Trace!" She fell to her knees. Tears came hot and quick.

Behind her Missus called to the panicked colonists, "It's all right. It's over. They've got their two."

Only then did Impani see a different group of ants carrying another man. She looked back, astounded to see the colonists still shrieking, still waving their arms, running back and forth.

Wouldn't they fight to rescue one of their own?

She hunched her shoulders. A horrible sense of hopelessness crashed over her. All the fear, all the dread she'd been hiding came out in one long wail.

Fingers pulled her to her feet.

"Come away from it," Missus said. "What were you thinking?"

"I hesitated," Impani cried. "I should have saved him."

Missus tugged her back into the paddock. "I'll make us a cup of tea."

Tea? How could she drink tea? "Where have they taken him?"

"Somewhere in the hive."

They turned at a sound behind them. A pair of soldiers picked up the ant Impani had killed.

"They eat their dead," Missus told her.

Sickness gnawed at Impani's stomach. This couldn't be real. As she crossed the yard, she glared at the now-silent colonists. "What is the matter with you people? Why don't you fight back?"

"Movement and noise confuse them," Missus said. "They'll take you if you hold still too long."

What kind of answer was that? "Maybe you should just hide."

"We tried. They ripped off the roofs looking for us. Did a lot of damage—and we lost a lot of friends." She motioned toward a small Quonset hut. "I live here."

Impani recoiled. "You have flowers on your windowsill?" Cheerful yellow pansies peeked through the window as if mocking her shock and horror.

"They clean the air. Go in." She pulled open the door.

Impani entered a sparse kitchen. Warmth enveloped her face. Lathi and Timothy peered at her from a doorway.

"Sit down. I put a kettle on before the attack."

Impani collapsed into a chair and cradled her head on the table. "I can't believe this is happening."

"I don't know what to tell you."

"Why would you even come to a planet like this?"

Missus shrugged. "We were all going to be rich. This world is a cornucopia of mineral deposits. When we landed, everything was perfect. The only hardship was the cold. We had an electric perimeter guard. At first we used it day and night, then only nights, and after a while not at all. Didn't seem to be a point. As far as we knew, we were the only ones here."

"That's what the Scouts told you?"

"They said they checked everything out." She poured two cups of tea. "Anyway, we had contracted for a supply drop to arrive one year after we'd landed. The ship was right on schedule. We were having a big one-year anniversary celebration, and we invited the captain and her crew.

"Then the soldiers attacked." She released a quavering breath. "Luckily, some of us thought to bring hunting rifles along. Bullets work well against them. For all their strength, they are rather fragile creatures. We forced them out of the paddock and raised the perimeter. The electric current kept them at bay, but even at full strength, it didn't kill them. We spent several months with soldiers constantly circling, testing the barrier."

"But you had the supply ship. You could have sent for help. Or drop everything and run."

"The pilot and some of the crew ran for the shuttle, but it was too far away. Soldiers caught them before they got half a klick. Later, we watched them dismantle the ship. We were trapped within our own encampment. So our project leader, Charlie Cummings, took one of the creatures captive. He wanted to try to communicate with it, find a way to cohabitate. I was amazed at how quickly it learned our language. We named it Kkrick."

"I've met him," Impani said.

"Kkrick told us there could be no peace. Ever. Because we were on their land. And if we moved a bit to the west, we would be on another tribe's land, and to the north someone else's. There was nowhere we could go. And all the while we were questioning Kkrick, the workers were tunneling beneath the encampment.

"They came up inside the perimeter. Soldiers flowed out of that hole. No matter how many we killed, there were always more. Finally, we ran out of ammunition. They slaughtered us. We started with one thousand colonists. Half died in that single battle."

"That's horrible."

"We didn't give up. We had the explosive charges we were using to sink wells. Charlie used them as weapons. He held the line while the rest of us gathered what we could and fled. We set up camp here." Missus stamped her foot. "Solid granite. They can't tunnel through. But the perimeter guard was damaged in the move. We lost a power coil." She paused to sip her tea. "The soldiers run a perimeter now—but this time it's to keep us in. We have no way to defend ourselves, so we just wait. They take us by twos."

"Every day?"

"No. Sometimes a month goes by. I think it depends on whether the queen is laying eggs."

Impani looked at her cooling cup. "I don't understand. You have power. Lights. Stoves. It's warm in here. So why can't you get the perimeter working?"

"Our generators run on solar power. It's limited, so we conserve energy by cutting everything but heaters at night. The perimeter guard is different. It pulls natural electricity from the air. Unlimited energy."

"Like my stat-gun."

"On a larger scale."

"But the coil itself is compatible." Impani held out her gun. "You only need to rig it to fit."

The woman's gaze took on a faraway cast. "It would cover a much smaller area. I'd have to move the relays closer together. But it might work."

"I'll give you the coil. In trade."

Missus raised a brow.

Impani leaned back in her chair. "Do you have more of those explosive charges?"

"We might."

"I want them. And whatever ammunition you may be hoarding."

Missus stared in a kind of appalled admiration. "You want to go after him, don't you? You want to go after Trace."

🪐 🪐 🪐

"I'm going after them," Natica told Ambri-Cutt outside the tech room. "And you're going to help me."

"All operations have been suspended. I'll lose my job," he said.

"That's not all you'll lose," she said, "after they find out you've been following Impani and leaving gifts at her door."

"That's drel. You'll never be able to prove it." He turned to walk away.

"Wait." Natica closed her eyes. "I'm sorry. It's just… She told me you were her friend."

"She did?"

"You're the only one who can do this. You have the power. I bet you've already worked out the calculations."

"They won't listen to me. But I know every world she's been to. I know where she'll be."

"Send me there. Help me rescue her."

Ambri-Cutt tugged at his lower lip. Natica read the desperation in his eyes—and guilt. He blamed himself for losing her.

"They'll recognize the energy drain," he muttered.

"We'll mask it. Somehow."

He paused then shook his head. "No. I can't send just one. The ring would be uneven. It would tear you apart."

"That's why I'm coming, too." Robert Wilde stepped into the hallway.

Natica folded her arms. "Robert, I–"

"Have no choice," he said. "Now, let's go get my girl."

❧ ❧ ❧

Impani slapped her hand on the kitchen table. "I have to get him. I can't let him be eaten by those... those–"

"And how do you plan to do that?" Missus said. "It's two klicks to the nearest hole. If you give your gun to us as you promised, you won't even have a weapon. How are you going to get past the patrols?"

She covered her face. "I don't know."

"Let's say by some miracle you do make it through them. What are you going to do then? Those tunnels are a maze. No one has ever come back out."

"You d-don't understand." Impani wept.

"Of course I do. He's your partner."

"He's m-more than my p-partner. He saved m-my life."

"And now you want to save his. But you're thinking like a young girl. It's time to grow up. Face the facts. Your partner is gone. You have to take care of yourself now." She placed her hand on her shoulder. "Give me the coil in your stat-gun, and in return I will give you a home as safe as any of ours."

She sat up and wiped her face. *I'm sorry Trace. So very, very sorry.*

"He would want you to be strong."

She sniffled and nodded.

"Good, then," Missus said. "Let's get that coil in place. Lathi, keep Timothy inside."

Wearily, Impani got up from the table and followed Missus out into the cold. The frigid air slapped her face.

Missus spread her arms. "This is your home, now."

What if it was? What if the ring never came for her again? How could she bear it without Trace?

She gazed at the bleached white stone and battered gray huts. Outside the perimeter, three spear-toting ants circled the paddock as if on guard duty. Their black shells shone in the sunlight. She sucked in her breath and shuddered. She couldn't let those monsters kill any more people.

She grabbed Missus' arm. "Do ants have ears?"

"No. They communicate with vibrations. That's why we were so surprised when Kkrick learned to speak."

"They're smart."

"Their leaders are. They have a caste culture. Why do you ask?"

"We need to make sure the camp is sitting on solid ground."

"I told you. Granite."

"I know. But once we have the perimeter back up, they'll be frantic to get back in here. Bugs can squeeze through the smallest cracks. If there's a fault line in the granite…"

Her face fell. "I didn't think of that."

"My resonator can map the area, but it uses sonic waves. I don't know how they'll react to the vibrations."

"It's worth the risk. Get ready. I'll tell you when they've moved far enough away."

Roxanne Smolen

Impani turned her back on the ants. She wanted to kill them, but she wasn't sure if she could take on three at once. Besides, Trace had warned about pheromones...

She closed her eyes. *Trace. What are they doing to you? Are you still alive?*

❧ ❧ ❧

As the bugs bore Trace through their tunnels, he fought to control his breathing. He had two choices: panic and become ant food, or wait for an opportune moment and fight.

Impani showed him how to kill the creatures: stun them first then slice them apart with a narrow beam at close quarters. The problem was he could kill only one at a time. He would have to make it the right one.

Without warning, the bugs tipped him from their shoulders into a narrow hole. He slid headfirst down a twisting chute and fell with a splash into fetid water. A second person fell on top of him. Trace leaped up, sputtering and coughing, and pulled the man to his feet.

They stood waist deep in warm, foul-smelling water. Yellow scum clung to their bodies. Trace spat and rubbed his stinging eyes. When would he learn to keep his mask in place?

The man hugged his arms and whimpered, walking in circles. Somehow, his fear made Trace feel calmer.

"What's your name?" Trace asked.

"Larry," he squeaked.

"Don't give up, Larry. We aren't dead yet."

They were at one end of a wide corridor. Black and red fissures branched over the stone, glowing like banked coals. The dark maws of tunnels dotted the walls. At the other end of the corridor, several torches decorated the mouth of a cave.

No one was in sight. Glancing about, Trace waded to the edge of the pool and climbed onto the rough bank.

He reached a hand to Larry. "Come on."

When they were both down, Trace tiptoed to the mouth of a tunnel. He took his flashlight from his belt and clipped it to his wrist. With a deep breath and a silent count of three, he leaped inside.

It wasn't a tunnel. It was a cave. A stockpile of rusted scrap metal. He saw posts and doors, even a pilot's chair.

"What the...?"

Larry bumped into his back. Trace spun around at a familiar clicking sound.

Two bugs stood behind them. They wore loose, colorless togas similar to the queen-feeders he'd met at the feast. Still clicking, they stepped into the cave.

"No! No!" Larry struggled as one lifted him and carried him into the corridor.

Hurriedly, Trace snapped his mask in place. If they were going to throw him back into that putrid pool, he wanted his face covered.

The bug recoiled as if confused by its reflection. In that instant, Trace blasted it with his stat-gun. It fell. Stunned. He narrowed the beam and shot it in the head. Ichor splashed the floor. Trace rushed out of the cave, determined to save Larry.

Larry wasn't alone. A half-dozen bugs had joined the one holding him.

A cloud of defeat settled over Trace. He lowered his head and holstered his gun. Bugs took his arms and marched him toward the torch-lit cave at the end of the hall. He leaned back, boots skidding as if he could stop them. He didn't want to know what was in there. Didn't want to die.

A shove sent him sprawling through the cave mouth. From his prone position, Trace looked up at the ant queen.

She shone jet-black and huge. Her long, segmented body hung from the ceiling by a birthing sack. Piles of pulsing, translucent eggs heaped the floor around her.

Slowly, barely breathing, Trace got to his feet. Her eyes followed his movement. Black. Fathomless. His flesh prickled beneath his skinsuit. He took out his gun. Beside him, Larry rose to his knees and rocked back and forth.

"Be ready to run," Trace whispered.

In a single rapid movement, he shot the queen then dove beneath her crackling body. Two feeders rushed through the door. On all six legs, they skittered toward him. He shot one. It fell covered in blue sparks. The other continued to advance.

The queen reared and thrashed as if shaking off the stunning effect of his weapon. She couldn't see him beneath her, so she struck out at what was nearest. The advancing bug. She lifted it into the air, ripped off its head then threw the body. It struck Trace in the chest and knocked him flat.

Lying beneath the decapitated carcass, he saw Larry steal out the door. He saw the first bug regain its feet. He fired again, but his aim was off. The energy ricocheted and struck a cache of eggs.

The shells exploded with brilliant flashes. The bug looked about as if amazed. Kicking out from cover, Trace strafed the floor with bolts of energy. The delicate eggs sizzled and burst, spewing their contents onto the floor.

With an ear-grating screech, the queen doubled over and looked directly at Trace. He saw his mask reflected in her black, glassy stare.

For a petrified moment, he froze. Then he fired between her eyes.

I mpani walked beside Missus, her attention upon her resonator. "Readings show the fault line receding in that direction. If you keep your perimeter guard on this side, there's no chance of the ants getting in."

"I'll put relays here and here." Missus shook her head. "I never thought to look for faults in the granite. You just saved us all."

"Yeah. I'm a real hero."

Missus stopped and glanced around. "What are they doing?"

The ants patrolling the outskirts of the paddock ran about on all six legs. They even climbed on top of one another.

Impani straightened and rested her hand on her holster. "Are they going to attack?"

"I'm not certain. I've never seen them act this way."

"Let's get those relays in position." She snapped the resonator onto her belt then waved at a group of colonists who stood staring at the ants. "Hey! Don't just stand there. Get everyone on this side of camp!"

Bedlam erupted as if she'd pulled a switch. People poured from their homes. They screamed and ran as frantically as the ants.

"Help me with this!" Missus wrestled a bulky dish across the yard.

Impani grabbed a rung and helped lug the relay over the rough ground. While Missus powered it up, she glanced at the colonists. Their haphazard scurrying alarmed her. She didn't want to shut anyone out when the perimeter went up.

"This way!" she shouted. "Over here!"

Missus grimaced. "My house is on the other side of the paddock. Out of the zone."

"I'll get the last relay in place. You get Lathi and Timothy. I'll meet you at the power station."

Missus ran off. Impani dragged the final dish. Metal squealed on stone. She cringed at the sound and glanced at the ants.

They crawled over one another in a mass of arms and legs. Snapping with their beaks. As if driven insane.

Then she noticed a much larger horde massing in the distance.

Chapter 12

Impani powered up the final relay. As she stood, she called to the fleeing colonists, "Over here! Get to this side of camp."

She watched them, bemused, then noticed that many people carried blankets and other supplies as they sprinted back and forth. Not quite as panic-stricken as she'd thought.

Dodging through the crowd, she searched for the power station. Then she saw it–a gray cube about a meter high. Missus ran toward her from the opposite direction. Her young son bounced in her arms. Lathi looked horrified.

Impani shouted, "The relays are in place."

"Give me your gun!" Missus slid Timothy down and dropped to her knees beside him. She opened the grip of the stat-gun.

The power coil nestled into red and white connectors. It looked much smaller than Impani had anticipated. What if it wasn't compatible with the perimeter coils after all? What would they do then?

She smacked the corners of the control panel with the heel of her hand, trying to open it, but grit and gravel had jammed it shut. With a grappling hook from her pack, she pried an edge. The panel popped, exposing an interior layered with thumbnail-sized circuit chips. They looked like a rainbow.

Missus tapped the gun's power unit into her palm. Stripping off the connectors, she hot-wired the coil into a spot for a component twice its size.

Impani winced with a sudden jab of panic. It wasn't going to work. They had to standardize the output. She studied the board, struggling to concentrate over the screams around her. "You should remove that shunt."

"No. We need it to channel excess energy to ground."

"But now you need to send any surplus to the smaller coil."

Missus glanced up. "This isn't the time to experiment."

"It will work." Impani brushed the woman's hands away and disconnected the shunt. "We'll set a jumper to keep it from arcing."

"Not bad. Did you learn that at your academy?"

"Some." She shrugged. "Mostly, I'm self-taught."

"That explains why you can think beyond the manual."

Shouts cut the din. "Soldiers! It's soldiers!"

Timothy whimpered and clung to his mother's coat.

Missus frowned. "Here they come."

Hundreds of ants swarmed toward them. But they didn't march like an army. They seemed disorganized, jostling each other, even climbing over one another in their effort to reach the compound. Skirmishes broke out. Blades flew.

Impani pulled her gaze back to the control panel. Her hands shook. She couldn't reach inside. "Give me a minute."

"We don't have a minute!"

She tore off her gloves and immediately regretted it. Her fingers numbed with the cold. Fumbling, she set the jumper. "Done!"

Missus flipped a lever. A rising whine joined the yells of the colonists. Impani sat back, scarcely breathing, staring at the approaching ants. Sunlight glinted from their spearheads, from the black orbs of their eyes. Then a flash encased the nearest ant. Another flash. The ants fell back.

"It's working," Missus whispered.

Impani stood. The camp blazed with brief flashes of light. The ants couldn't get through the perimeter guard. "We did it."

"You did it," Missus told her. Tears shone in her eyes.

The alarmed cries of the colonists grew into a deafening cheer. People converged upon them, hugging Missus and slapping Impani on the back.

Smiling and nodding distractedly, Impani pulled on her gloves and tucked her frozen hands into her armpits. She watched the ants beyond the barrier.

The frenzied creatures battered the guard. Fights broke out among them. Suddenly they were slaughtering one another. Blades sang. Beaks sank into mid-sections. The white stone ran with yellow blood.

The cheer fell.

"What are they doing?"

"They're killing each other."

"Keep this up, and there will be no more ants to fear."

"There will always be more ants. If this tribe falls, another will take its place."

Impani looked at them. They huddled together, as afraid as they'd ever been. They should never have been sent to this world. It was a mistake. A Scouting mistake. At least with the perimeter guard repaired, the colony had a chance.

A sob hiccupped in her chest. If she had saved Trace, they would have had a chance, too.

🪐 🪐 🪐

Trace crawled out from beneath the huge queen ant. Her head had exploded. He backed away, staring, wiping yellow goo from his mask.

From behind him, a bug wrapped its spindly arms about his chest. Trace threw back his head but was unable to strike the creature. He flipped forward, hoping to throw it off, but the bug tightened its grip. Cutting him in two.

The bug jerked and twisted. Something splashed Trace's neck. It jerked again then fell. Trace grasped his chest and turned around.

Larry swung a lead pipe and bashed in the bug's head. Gore dripped from his clothing as if he'd been on a killing spree.

"Thanks," Trace wheezed.

"Found this in the stockpile." He panted. "Don't know why we didn't think of using good old fashioned clubs before."

"Let's get out of here."

But before they could reach the cave mouth, a ruckus sounded outside. Ants poured into the corridor. At least fifty of them. They crawled the walls and each other.

Then blood began to fly.

"What the–" Trace flattened against the wall and peered out. "It's a riot."

"Why would they attack other ants?"

"I think I started a war when I killed the queen. Unless another queen steps forward, they'll keep on killing."

"What should we do? Wait until they're all dead?"

"That could take days. And if the fighting should spill into here…" Trace glanced about the cave. His old ant farm swam to mind. "Wait. There's always another entrance into the queen's chambers. An air hole in case the tunnel collapses."

He followed the cave wall, stepping gingerly over broken eggs and body parts.

Larry went the opposite way. "Here. I think I've found it."

"Good job." Trace hurried to him and shone a light up the narrow, slanted tunnel. He took out his gun. "I'll go first. Stay close."

🪐 🪐 🪐

Impani walked at Missus' side. She felt like second in command. The colonists watched them intently. Now that the camp was smaller, the paddock felt crowded.

"We need an accounting of supplies," Missus called. "And some of us have lost our homes, so we'll have to double up."

"We should get a head count, too," Impani said in a low voice. "If anyone was caught outside when that perimeter went up, we'll need to stage a rescue."

"You're right," Missus said. "I'm glad you're here, Miss Fix."

Impani smiled. Then a familiar twist jerked her stomach. She gasped.

The Impellic ring was coming.

What should she do? Should she take off her belt and refuse to leave? It was a horrible planet, but at least there were people. Who knew where she'd jump to next.

But what if Trace was still alive? Should she let the ring take her and hope it picked him up, too? Would it even find him underground?

Missus touched her shoulder. "Impani, what's wrong?"

She backed away. "I have to go."

"You're leaving? Now?"

"I'm sorry."

Missus held her son, the boy's small arms about her neck—and for a moment, Impani wanted to hug them, let the ring take all three of them away from this hideous world. But she remembered the creature from the forest-fire planet. The ring could carry only two.

"I swear, if I get back to Base, I'll send help," Impani said.

Missus nodded. "I know you will."

Then darkness blotted out the woman's face, erased the camp as if it had never been.

Impani screwed up her face against a bout of tears. How could she leave those poor people? How could she not? Her body stretched, and her very molecules threatened to burst.

Please let the ring find Trace. Please don't let him be dead.

A solid blow drove out all thought. She hit the ground rolling. A caustic gasp blistered her throat. With a strangling noise, she clutched her neck, eyes streaming, stomach clenched.

Numbly, she fastened her mask. She tried to breathe, concentrated upon taking a single breath, but for a terrifying moment, she couldn't make her lungs work. Liquid fire coursed through her veins. Her limbs twitched. Muscles twisted into painful knots. She rolled onto her side and cradled her chest.

"Trace," she said hoarsely as if her throat were shredding. Lifting onto her elbows, she called as loudly as she could, "Trace!"

The sky flashed, and the ground shook with thunder. She sat, feeling queasy and weak. She was alone. Her partner was not in sight.

"Trace," she whispered.

Why hadn't the ring picked him up? Had he been too deep beneath the stone for the homing beacon to penetrate? Had the ants taken off his belt? What if he was in that hive right now, waiting for her, expecting her to rescue him?

She drew her knees to her chest. Tears spattered her mask. She should have stayed behind to look for him. He was her partner. Partners stick together. But even as she thought it, she knew he was much more. He was brave and smart and... he was gone.

She struggled to her feet. Shades of orange painted the landscape with jagged boulders and rough hills. Flaked rock covered the ground like rust. Overhead, a gas-giant planet filled the sky with muted bands of brown.

She saw no life at all. She was alone.

Suddenly she leaned forward, seized by a fit of coughing. Breath raged in her throat. Her chest felt crushed in a vice.

She checked the environmental sensors on her sleeve. The atmosphere was oxygen-based but with enough toxins to poison her. She would have died with prolonged exposure.

When would she learn to keep her mask in place?

Hands on her knees, she caught her breath. A whining sound drew her attention. Beneath the skinsuit, her flesh prickled.

The world flashed inferno red. A lightning bolt knocked her off her feet. Searing heat shot through her skinsuit. The ground shook and split. A jagged fissure grew where the bolt had struck. Fragments of rock peppered her mask.

Impani ran. Thunder boomed around her. Thick bolts of electricity spiked the ground and branched overhead like tree limbs. Rock flew with each strike. Rifts opened, some over a meter in width. She leaped across, her breath rasping painfully, legs shaking. Her skin tingled with countless minute shocks.

Then a bolt struck nearly on top of her, encasing her in electric brilliance. The world teetered. Her boots slid as the ground dropped. She twisted, fighting the fall, flailing her arms. The fissure opened wider and swallowed her.

She landed on her back with a loud *oof.* Darkness was absolute. She raised a hand to her mask. She couldn't see it, couldn't tell if her eyes were open or closed.

Where was the light? How far had she fallen? Was it ten meters or one hundred? She gasped, arms outstretched against the blackness. Thunder shook the rock. It sounded muffled and dull.

I'm blind. The lightning—

Panic erupted from the back of her throat. "Help me!" she screamed. "Somebody help!"

246

Memories enveloped her, and she was again a young girl trapped in a trash compactor. She felt the rawness of her throat once more, felt fear-sweat on her brow—and the horrific touch of unseen creatures moving. Slithering.

But I'm not a young girl. I'm a cadet.

She slowed her breathing until she could no longer hear it. Searching her belt, she took out her flashlight.

Something touched her shoulder.

Her heart froze mid-beat. Stop it! You're imagining things. She switched on the lamp.

It wouldn't light. She clapped it against her palm, her pulse rising like a siren. Fear tickled the back of her neck.

No. Not fear. Something touched her.

She gasped and wrested away. Cold fingers clenched her stomach. Something moved in the dark.

Wide-eyed, she waited.

Gently, a tentacle drifted around her neck. She knocked it away, touching it, feeling it and yet not feeling it, as if it were the darkness itself reaching for her, pulsing, entwining. Panic stripped her mind. She kicked blindly, striking nothing, trying to turn, to crawl away.

Darkness enfolded her in its many arms, tendrils slinking over her, thick pulsing worms winding about her body, sliding, writhing. Consciousness slipped as if her mind took a step back, disconnecting from the horror even as her body sank deeper. Terror gurgled in her throat.

A glove pierced the dark.

"Grab on!" Trace yelled.

Impani blinked. She reached for the hand, felt it tighten about her fingers, pulling her. The darkness resisted, would not set her free. She heard a wet, sucking sound, and then dim light broke over her. She gasped, kicking hard, scrambling upward as if she'd been drowning, crawling from the hole that was three meters deep, not ten, not one hundred. She hadn't fallen far at all. She rolled onto the surface and sobbed.

Lightning flashed. She could barely see it. Thick, black mucous covered her mask.

Trace shook her. "We have to go."

Thunder rent the air.

Impani stammered. "There was something d-down there."

"I know. I saw it."

"What? You saw what?" She stared, and then her mouth dropped open. "Trace! You're here! You're alive!" She hugged him tightly. "I wanted to look for you, but Missus was making tea and– How did you find me?"

"I followed the screams."

"I was screaming?"

"Come on. There's shelter over here."

He wrapped his arm about her shoulder, supporting her, forcing her to move. She staggered. Was it a dream? Was he really there with her? She concentrated upon placing one foot before the other. Lightning split the sky, and she ducked from the erupting thunder.

They reached a pile of boulders and sat beneath an outcropping. Impani couldn't stop shivering. She swiped at the mucous on her mask, smearing it.

"I thought I'd never see you again." She sniffled.

"I killed the queen," he blurted as if bursting to tell her.

She paused, thinking slowly. "You killed the—"

"Just like you showed me. Got up close and shot her in the head."

"That must be why the ants were acting so weird."

"You saw that, too?"

"Yeah. They were about to attack. I got the perimeter guard up just in time."

He cocked his head. "How did you fix their perimeter guard?"

"I used the power coil from my stat-gun." She braced for his admonishment. Now they were short a weapon.

But he gave her a slow smile. "Brilliant."

She blushed and looked away. "It made me consider our situation. If I could get more power to the homing device, it might realign the rings."

"How do we go about doing that?"

"We could take the power core from the homing unit in my belt and hotwire it into yours. Then if you could hold me really tight and not let go–"

"Not a problem," he said.

He pulled her close and rested his cheek on the top of her head. She relaxed into his embrace. Lightning lit the crevice, and the rocks trembled around her.

"What was that thing with me in the hole?" she murmured.

"Just a black, shapeless mass. Reminded me of an amoeba with cilia around its nucleus. I had to punch through–you were completely encased. I'm surprised you had air."

An alien life form, probably living off minerals in the rocks, giving off oxygen as a bi-product. The darkness hadn't come alive, hadn't been reaching for her. A twinge of embarrassment heated her cheeks. She gazed from their meager shelter at the orange plains beyond.

Suddenly she sat upright. "Is someone out there?" She stared, not daring to believe.

Two figures came into view–one with a familiar gait.

"Natica?"

Chapter 13

Trace stared in confusion as Impani crawled from beneath the awning of rocks and stood in the open.

"It's Natica." She bounced like a schoolgirl. "My friend, Natica Galos."

He was about to assert that he didn't see anyone when suddenly he did. Two figures climbed down a ridge. Their skinsuits reflected the orange rock, making them almost invisible. He pulled out the tri-views and focused until he could see the shimmer of their masks.

"They found us," he murmured, not ready to believe until he heard it from his own lips. He slid out to stand beside Impani, whooping and waving. "Over here!"

One of the figures waved back.

"Come on!" Impani tugged his arm then ran.

He had to hustle to catch up. Lightning arced overhead and the ground shook—and part of him thought they were crazy to be out in the open like this.

They reached the bottom of the ridge. Boulders barred their way. Trace led through a narrow pass. The trail steepened until he was climbing the rock face by fingertip, digging with the toes of his boots. His chest heaved in the heavy air. A lightning strike bombarded him with shards, and the resounding thunder felt almost physical.

At last, he reached the top of the boulder. He stretched out his hand for Impani. An avalanche of pebbles rained down. He gazed upward at two Scouts upon a ledge.

"Natica!" Impani called.

Her friend laughed as if in relief. "Pani!"

Just then, a bolt of lightning struck at the Scouts' feet. Through the glare, Trace saw one of them fly backward. The other toppled into a widening rift.

"No!" Impani screamed.

Trace climbed with a burst of energy. He reached the ledge just as the first Scout staggered to his feet.

"Are you hurt?" Trace grasped his arm to steady him.

He wrenched his arm away.

Impani fell to her knees beside the jagged crevasse. "Oh, no. Can either of you see her?"

Trace unclipped his wrist lamp. He played the light over rough, broken rock. The opening was narrow. Less than a meter wide. But the hole ran deep.

"There." He passed his light over a silvery skinsuit. "She isn't moving."

"Oh God. Don't let her be dead."

"Hello, Impani," said the other Scout.

"Robert." Her voice was breathy. Then she seemed to collect herself. She looked again into the hole. "We have to get her out of there."

Trace looked at the Scout, recognizing him. Robert Wilde, ringleader of a band of thugs. There was someone like him in every school. Even in prison.

"What should we do?" she cried. "There's no telling what else is down there with her."

"What are you talking about?" Wilde shouted over a crash of thunder. "She's stuck in a rock. What else *could* be with her?"

Impani's expression hardened. "I'll get her."

"No. I will," Trace said.

She pulled a length of line from her belt and snapped a hook to the end.

He took her hands in his. "It's all right. You don't have to."

"She's my friend." Tears quavered behind her voice. "Besides, I'm the only one small enough." Her gaze held his for a moment. Then she thrust the line into his hand. "Don't let go."

"Depend on it." He watched her lower herself over the edge. Black ichor still streaked her mask. "Here." He clipped his lamp onto her wrist.

She smiled then climbed into darkness.

"How touching." Wilde sneered. He said something more, but thunder drummed out his words.

Trace watched Impani's bobbing light as she fed out the line. He entwined his fingers with the tines of the hook. "So, what's the plan? How do we get out of here?"

"The plan's gone down headfirst," Wilde said. "Galos had the equipment and the instructions."

Trace's stomach sank. "I suppose you're along just to balance the ring."

"I came to deliver a message." Wilde leaned nearer. "Stay away from Impani. She's mine."

"What?"

"You heard. She's scared and confused right now, and I'm sure you took advantage of that. But when we get back to the academy, things will be how they were. That means without you."

Trace stared, thunderstruck. Could Impani be involved with this raffer? "You're nuts." He hoped to sound unconcerned. But inside, his emotions churned. Had he misread Impani's interest?

The line slackened.

Impani called, "I've reached her."

"Is she breathing?"

"I think so. Not much room to move down here. I can't get a good hold." She paused. "All right. I'm retracting the line."

Trace braced himself, holding on with both hands.

Wilde jostled him. "I'll take it."

"What? Get away!" He pushed back.

"She's my girl. I'll pull her up." Wilde grabbed the line.

"We can discuss this when they're safe."

A crashing blow to the side of Trace's head sent him sprawling. He struggled to keep his grip on Impani's line. Wilde leaped onto his chest, grabbed his shoulders, and shook him until his head rattled against the ground.

Trace struck out with his free arm. Arching his back, he tossed Wilde to the side. Wilde rose to hands and knees and then mule-kicked him in the face. Trace's head snapped back. His ears rang. Dazed, he lifted his fingers to his mask. The hook dropped from his hand.

🪐 🪐 🪐

Impani wedged her back against the wall, gazing upward at the mouth of the crevice as the guide line yanked her belt. "Hey. What's going on up there?"

Lightning flashed and tossed brief outlines around her. She hoisted her friend higher upon her shoulder and continued to scale the jagged breach.

Abruptly, the retracting mechanism on her belt whirred. She gazed upward, gaping as the line trailed toward her.

❧ ❧ ❧

Trace dove for the line. He missed it by centimeters. The hook dragged along the ground then disappeared. He grunted as Wilde's elbow slammed into his ribcage. Rage filled him. He got to his knees. "You idiot! You let her fall!"

"You let her fall," Wilde said, "and she'll know it was you."

Trace punched him in the face so hard he thought his hand broke. Thunder cracked like a sonic whip. He crept to the edge of the fissure and stared into darkness. The light was gone. Where was Impani?

Wilde barreled into him. They rolled, grappling for position, finally coming to rest with Wilde on top and Trace's head hanging off the ledge. Wilde's fist pressed beneath Trace's jaw. The edge crumbled beneath his shoulders. Trace locked his arms about him, determined to take Wilde with him if he fell.

Then he felt a familiar twist of his gut. Vertigo broke in waves. The Impellic ring was coming to claim him. He writhed, gasping beneath Wilde's chokehold, trying to tell him, trying to warn him away.

The void pounced like a living entity.

Newton Ambri-Cutt leaped from his seat and whirled about as Chief Astrut burst into the control room.

"What are you doing?" the Chief yelled. "Operations are suspended."

Ambri-Cutt backed away. "You've got two cadets out there—"

"Now, I've got four!" He spread his arms. "Did you think this experiment of yours would go undetected?"

"I can bring her home. I know I can."

"Without authorization? What were you thinking?"

Squaring his shoulders, Ambri-Cutt said, "I was thinking that the lives of those two young people were worth losing my job."

"Oh, you've gone far beyond losing your job. This is a government installation. You'll be lucky if you aren't tried for treason."

Ambri-Cutt cringed. He hadn't thought of that, hadn't considered the consequences at all. He only wanted to see Impani safe.

The Chief pushed past him and sat at the control panel.

"Wait!" Ambri-Cutt cried.

"This mission ends now. I'm recalling your rescue team."

"But they are already on the planet. I know they can find them."

"In theory." The Chief's fingers flitted over the panel. "Your theory."

Ambri-Cutt watched with mounting despair as the chromed cylinder brightened and illuminated the Impellic Chamber. Maybe it will be all right. Maybe they had time to give Impani the equipment.

He squinted into the glare. The light intensified then cut. His jaw dropped. Taking a shaky step forward, he stared at the Chamber.

The ring was empty.

Robert Wilde blinked into yellow sunlight. He rolled from Trace Hanson's prone form and gazed at a green-blue sky. He stared at a whitewater river.

Why hadn't he returned to the Chamber?

He stiffened, at once amazed and enraged.

"You dragged me with you." He rammed his boot into Hanson's ribcage.

Hanson groaned, slow to respond.

Wilde got to his feet and paced. It wasn't supposed to happen this way. He'd planned to take Impani back with him, leave Hanson and Galos stranded. He looked down at Hanson. The raffer had spoiled everything.

Hanson held his chest. Wilde hoped he'd cracked a few of his ribs.

Then Hanson cried, "Impani!" and ran off down the bank.

Only then did Wilde notice two heads bobbing in the rapids.

Impani gasped as water closed over her head. Her mask felt oddly weighted. She lifted her chin, searching for the surface. The undertow sent her somersaulting. The force of the current threatened to tear Natica from her grasp. With her friend tight in her arms, she rebounded from the river bottom and aimed toward the light.

Bright sky. Whitewater. She slammed the rocks, helpless in the current. Noise muffled and roared as she fought to keep the surface, fought to keep Natica's head up. Water tossed them like flotsam. She glanced toward a shoreline, toward bushes and trees, and saw someone running.

Trace!

She tried to call to him, but the river sucked her under and pitched her end over end. Her mask grew heavy, the filters sodden. She burst again into the tumult of the water. Bobbing. Struggling. For a brief moment, she saw the sky. Then the weight of the mask pulled her under. In the back of her mind, a voice warned that she was running out of air.

The crosscurrent scooped her onto her back and tossed her into daylight. She glimpsed a wedge of rock before sinking beneath the surface. Sound became distant. Her vision dimmed. A peculiar heaviness built in her chest.

Suffocating. Have to get the mask off. She raised her hands. Natica slipped away and edged deeper.

"No!" Impani dove then wrapped her friend in a tight embrace. "I've got you."

She closed her eyes and listened to her breath, ragged and hollow. The world became still.

Then sound broke around her, slapping her awake. Rocks loomed ahead, misty shapes in raging water. She thrashed against the current. Tumbling.

A sudden jerk snapped her around. She leaned into the tautness of her safety line and saw Trace standing in the churning river, one boot against the rocks, holding the end of the line. Water coursed over her, tugging, ripping. The pressure of her belt cut into her ribs.

A hand closed over her forearm. Impani startled, eyelids fluttering, then winced at the pull upon her arm. She grimaced, nearly torn in two by the weight on her other arm–the weight of her friend.

Gritting her teeth, she heaved Natica upward. The burden left her. The pain ceased. She felt only the tug of her belt. Like a tether. Water washed over her.

Cold air exploded against her face. She gasped and doubled over, coughing. The river spat at her. Water burned her eyes. Firm hands pulled her higher upon the wedge of rock.

Numbly, she wondered who had removed her mask. She glanced up. "Robert?"

"Relax," Robert said. "You're safe."

"Where's Natica?"

"I've got her."

She leaned into his arms, her body spent, ears pounding with the roar of the rapids. Then she saw Trace.

She held out her hand for his. "Trace, thank you. Thank you both."

He tossed her the hook from her safety line, his expression hidden by his spattered mask. "Let's get out of this river." He lifted Natica like a child and waded to the bank.

Impani gaped, taken aback, and followed her partner. She buried her hands in curly gray grass and pulled herself out of the water.

For a moment, she only lay there, breathing in the musty fragrance of the alien world. Then she crawled to Natica. She winced at her friend's pallor. But she was alive.

Trace unlatched his mask, and slid it to the top of his head. He looked exhausted. She wanted to ask what had happened to him while she was in the crevice. What made him let go of the line?

But Robert pushed between them. "This is the wrong world. I'm not supposed to be here."

Impani nodded. "I know why Natica came over. I was holding her as tightly as I could. But I don't know why you–" She stared. Had they been fighting? Had they been grappling around in the dirt when the ring came for Trace?

"Well, somebody better figure something out," Robert said. "How could a ring pick up four of us, anyway? I thought they could only carry two."

"Where's the equipment you mentioned?" Trace growled.

"Here." Robert rummaged through Natica's belt and pulled out two drenched parcels. He paused then looked up, eyes wide, voice low. "The power pack is missing."

Chapter 14

Trace glared. "What exactly do you mean, missing?"

"I mean the modules are gone," Wilde said. "Some of her other stuff, too. Her gun. Her med-pac. The device we used to find you."

"Drel! They must be in the river."

"Don't blame me," said Wilde. "You're the reason they were in the water in the first place."

"Me?" he shouted.

"If you hadn't dropped them—"

"Robert, this isn't helping," Impani said.

"I'm not even supposed to be here," he growled and folded his arms.

Trace opened the end of a parcel. Circuit chips. He handed them to Impani. "See what you can do with this."

"First, we have to help Natica."

"Oh, by all means. Let's help Natica." He snapped open his med-pac and tossed vials onto the pale grass. "We have an antigen, an analgesic, a general antitoxin. Which of these do you think will help?"

She stared at him, and he felt like a jerk.

"Impani, I think she has a head injury. The best way to help her is to get her back home to a hospital. Please look at the components."

"You just don't get it, do you?" Wilde leaped to his feet. "The power pack is missing. The components are worthless."

"What were they supposed to do?" She poured thumbnail-sized chips into her hand.

"Recall the ring or something. I don't know." Then he added hotly, "Galos said she understood, so why should I bother?"

"Right," Trace said. "You were just along for the ride."

Wilde's eyes flashed, and muscles rippled along his jaw. Trace stood slowly, his gaze unwavering.

With a derisive sniff, Wilde turned his back. "I'm going to see if anything washed up downstream."

Trace watched him walk away. He glanced at Impani, and before he could consider his words, he blurted, "You're going out with him?"

She blushed. "I've tried to break it off, but he won't listen. When I saw him with Natica just now, I thought that he was stalking me all the way out here."

Her sincerity deflated his anger. He relaxed his stance. She opened the second package, taking out a larger circuit board and setting it on the grass. He watched her, wanting to tell her how important she'd become to him, that he wanted to be the one with her.

"I'm sorry I dropped you," he said. "When I saw you in that river–"

"It's all right."

"No it's not. I let you down. You have a right to be angry."

"I'm too hungry to be mad. But I found a flaw in our facemasks. The filters became so water-logged I could barely lift my head."

"We'll have to complain about that when we get back."

Her shoulders sagged. "We're never getting back. I have no idea what to do with this board."

He searched for something insightful to say. Silence stretched between them. He glanced down the river just as a silvery, oblong shape cleared the trees. "What's that?"

Impani leaped up. "It's an airship. If there's civilization here, maybe they can help Natica."

He peered through his field glasses. "It's a hot air balloon. I see several people. They're...

273

throwing things overboard. And someone on the ground is shooting back at them. Darts or maybe small arrows."

"It's a battle?"

Had they dropped into a war zone? He focused upon the people on the balloon. They were throwing heavy-looking round objects. Like cannonballs only without the cannon.

"We need to find cover," he said. "Gather up the circuit chips. I'll get Natica."

"What about Robert?"

Trace ignored the question. Lifting Natica, he led away from the riverbank. The thunder of the rapids receded. Corkscrew-shaped reeds clattered as they walked beneath the trees. Gnarled, leafless branches formed a lattice overhead.

"They won't see us here." He set Natica upon the damp ground.

"Maybe they should see us," Impani said. "Maybe they have cities and doctors."

"I'd like that. But rings are programmed to drop onto uninhabited planets. If there were cities in evidence, we wouldn't be here."

Impani nodded dejectedly. She looked drained. Kneeling beside her unconscious friend, she asked, "Why won't she wake?"

"I think she's in shock. The skinsuit will keep her warm."

"We have to do something."

"I'm afraid of making it worse."

Her face contorted. A sob escaped her, and she put a hand to her mouth. "I can't have anyone else die because of me."

"What do you mean?"

She shook her head. "Nothing. Never mind."

"Come on. What is it?"

Her mouth worked soundlessly for a moment. "I can't tell you."

He put his arm around her. "I know about secrets. They start out as fear, but with time

275

and silence, they grow into something more. The only way to control them is to tell one person. Someone you trust."

She nodded against his chest. He pulled her closer, content to wait until she felt ready to speak. Then he heard footsteps crashing through the brush behind him.

🪐 🪐 🪐

Impani felt a jab of irritation as Trace pulled away. She'd been ready to tell him—wanted to tell him, wanted him to understand. She looked over his shoulder to see Robert Wilde running toward them through the crooked trees. Her cheeks warmed and she shied from Trace's side, which only made her angrier. She wouldn't let Robert control her life.

Then she saw the panic on his face.

"There you are!" Robert cried. "Get up! We've got to go."

Foreboding filled her hollow stomach. She stood as several purple-skinned humanoids stepped out from behind the trees and surrounded them.

They were at least two and a half meters tall and had narrow, sloping shoulders. Their hair was thick, white, and bristled like a mane. Chainmail covered their torsos, but their feet were bare. They wore miniature crossbows strapped to their wrists.

"Warriors," she whispered.

Trace made a disgusted sound at Robert. "You led them to us?"

"Right." Robert scowled. "Considering I didn't know where you had gone."

"Shush." Impani glared at the boys then stepped forward. "We are peaceful travelers. We mean no harm."

One of the warriors made a sound crossed between a goose and a donkey. He moved as if he were made of rubber. The others pointed their crossbows. She became acutely aware of her empty holster.

Still honking and braying, the purple alien walked up to her and shoved her hard. Trace leaped between them.

As Impani staggered backward, Robert drew his stat-gun. "Don't!" she shouted.

Before he could fire, a warrior sprang in a textbook Karate spin and kicked the gun from his hand. The first warrior picked it up. Trace dove into her, knocking her to the ground as a bolt of energy shot overhead. A severed tree limb and many twisted twigs rained down.

She rose to her knees. The alien held the stat-gun with confidence, as if familiar with it.

Trace whispered, "How did he know how to fire a weapon?"

She shook her head. It didn't make sense. Why wear a coat of mail but no helmet, no boots? Why bother with arrows if you could wield a gun?

The first warrior pulled her up, shoving her and waving his rubbery arms.

She pushed back and shouted, "I can't go with you. I have an injured companion."

As if planned, several aliens placed Natica on the tree limb that had fallen with the blast. They dragged her into the woods.

"Hey! Stop!" she yelled. A solid shove caused her to gulp and cough. The purple warrior towered over her. Impani sorted through her options and realized she had very few. Falling in line with the other warriors, she hurried after Natica.

Behind her, Robert muttered, "Nice move, Hanson. You know you can't fight."

"I'm not the one who gave them a gun," Trace told him.

Impani hissed between her teeth. "Stop it! Both of you!"

"But you'd think he'd never been trained in first-contact situations," Trace said.

She shot him a furious glance. As far as first-contact scenarios went, this was a disaster.

The purple-skinned warriors marched them at a steady pace through the woods. Tangled grass snagged her boots. She noticed no other creatures on the ground, but the trees harbored black-and-green snakes. She also saw small, long-tailed marsupials that watched with golden eyes as the group passed beneath their nests.

The sun dipped low. Rays flashed through the naked branches. Her breath frosted with the plummeting temperature. She trembled with hunger. Taking out her flask of water, she drank deeply, hoping to fill the gnawing emptiness within her.

She imagined Trace's disapproving gaze at her back. They would need the water. She didn't care. She only had to wait until Natica awoke. Natica would know what to do with the circuit board. She would get them home.

They stepped into a clearing ringed by tree stumps. A wooden tower with a lookout perch stood in the center. Large, sloping mounds scalloped the ground. A purple person crawled out of one, and Impani realized the mounds were houses made of living grass, the stringy, matted strands combed over low frames.

The person hooted and pointed. Suddenly, the glade swarmed with purple-skinned people. Some wore coats of mail like warriors, but most were naked. They flapped their rubbery arms as if shooing the cadets away.

Children ran from the houses. They walked in step with Impani and her captors, looking up as if in awe. Their stomachs were distended, their bodies tinted violet by the light of the setting sun.

The warriors halted and surrounded the cadets as if to keep them from running away. The one with Robert's gun hurried ahead and disappeared inside a grassy mound.

Impani glanced about the village. Fish dried on a rack over a smoky fire. Another rack held wooden rakes probably used to maintain the grass huts. She saw nothing to indicate an aggressive society.

People clustered around her, watching with hooded eyes. They hooted softly. Then the purple warrior fairly flew out of the hut. Impani gawped at a man who emerged.

He had long, tangled hair and a beard to mid-chest, looking like a man marooned on a desert island. He wore a skinsuit with the hood pulled back.

"Friends!" He laughed, arms spread wide. "Welcome to the end of the line."

Chapter 15

Impani stared at the wild-looking man. "You're a Scout."

He bowed flamboyantly. "My name is Joss. But you may refer to me as Your Royal Emperor."

"What?" She blinked.

Robert made a broad gesture. "You're leader here?"

Joss widened his eyes. "All mine. And these are my *grapes*."

Grapes? Was that what he called the purple-skinned humanoids? Impani took a step back and bumped into the *grape* behind her.

283

The first warrior held out Robert's stat-gun and hooted as if relaying a story.

Joss took the gun, turning it over in his hands, whispering. "Refit date. Refit date." Suddenly, he whooped and leaped into the air. "Where are the rest? I want all the firearms."

Trace hesitated. As if prodded, he stepped forward and handed over his stat-gun.

"That's all?" Joss looked crestfallen. Then he grinned. "I see our government has wisely decided to issue empty holsters to females."

Robert chuckled.

Joss checked the weapon then yelled, "Yes! I have survived another year! I reign supreme!" He hopped in a circle, waving the guns and shooting into the air. Abruptly, he tossed them back to Trace and Robert. "This calls for a celebration. A luau! Everyone will attend!"

Impani stared as he honked instructions to the villagers. She pointed. "Our friend is hurt."

"No excuses!" he bellowed.

He stormed off, braying and gesturing. Villagers and warriors alike rushed to his call. The cadets were left alone at the edge of the village.

"This is creepy," she whispered.

"I know." Robert nodded. "What are the odds of finding another lost Scout? How often do Impellic rings malfunction, anyway?"

He sounded relieved. Perhaps he felt that if Joss could survive on this planet, he could, too. But she wasn't so sure. Joss acted mentally unbalanced.

"What did he mean," she asked, "when he called this place the end of the line?"

૨ ૨ ૨

Newton Ambri-Cutt entered the tribunal hall, glancing at the vast ceiling as if he would be struck down at any moment. His footsteps echoed unevenly. Clearing his throat, he sat at the end of a large T-shaped table. The cross section was elevated so that the seven Board members looked down upon him. He felt like an insect under glass.

The Chairman said, "Please sit back and rest your hands on the arms of the chair. This shouldn't take long." He raised his voice. "Begin recording."

A spotlight clicked, affixing to Ambri-Cutt's face. Wincing, he glanced down the table at Director Hammond, hoping for a nod of support, a promise of help. Her gray eyes showed no emotion.

The Chairman said, "This is a preliminary hearing into charges of gross misconduct by Technician First Class, Newton Ambri-Cutt. Mr. Ambri-Cutt, are you aware of the systems lockdown at the academy?"

Ambri-Cutt sought his voice. "Yes, sir."

"And did you willfully disregard that order?"

"I did, sir," he said. "Yes."

A murmur of voices swept the Board. Then a woman leaned forward. Her dark hair was pulled back so severely, her eyebrows looked perpetually surprised.

"As a technician," she said, her voice high-pitched and grating, "are you aware of the enormous cost of maintaining an Impellic field?"

He shifted in his seat. "I know it's a bit expensive, but–"

"Yet you took it on yourself to design and initiate an unsanctioned ring sequence. What happened to the ring in question?"

"It came back empty."

"Empty." She nodded. "The children you sent are dead."

She waited as if expecting him to answer, and he choked back the words that came to mind. *What about the children you sent out? What about Impani? You discontinued the rescue to save your budget.*

Director Hammond's voice broke into the silence. "Mr. Ambri-Cutt, did you sabotage the session in which Purveyor Aldus Hanson's son was lost?"

"No. Of course I didn't."

"Are you a sympathizer with the movement to end the colonial program?"

He gaped at her, cold shock sliding down his shoulder blades. She was going to do it, just as she said she would. She was going to use him as a scapegoat. "You know I'm not."

She gave a chilling smile. "Why did you disregard the order to suspend operations?"

He folded his arms. "Rescue."

"Please keep your hands on the arms of the chair," the Chairman told him.

Ambri-Cutt jerked. He squirmed from the spotlight then lowered his arms.

"Could you repeat your reply?" Hammond asked.

He glared at her. "I wanted to save them."

"They are lost in a wormhole. Where in this universe did you plan to look?"

"I back-loaded the beacon, developed a process—"

"A process that had never been used before," she said. "A process that had never even been thought of before until you conceived it."

He stared in silence, gripping the arms of his chair. He hoped they were getting a good reading, hoped they knew how murderous he felt at that moment.

Hammond sat back. "In good faith, I authorized one rescue mission. Can you tell us what happened to that mission?"

"It failed."

"And yet you felt confident enough to refine your computations and try again—risking all this?" She motioned dramatically. "Mr. Ambri-Cutt, do you know how many training missions we have lost in this manner?"

"Three in the ten years I've been here."

"Do you know how many scouting missions the CEB has lost?"

"I don't know. One or two."

"Per year, Mr. Ambri-Cutt. One or two missions per year. Costly, as my colleague has pointed out, not only in energy waste but also in man-hours, training, and public sentiment. A process to track and retrieve lost Scouts would be invaluable."

Just then, the door opened. A man and a woman entered the room. They sat at the end of the table near Ambri-Cutt.

Director Hammond said, "I've invited Mr. Morimoto and Miss Johnston to this hearing. As observers only, of course."

The Chairman slapped the tabletop. "This is highly irregular."

Hammond's voice turned colder than her eyes. "What is irregular, Mr. Chairman, is that this Board would vote to disband and then deem to sit in judgment of a man for disregarding orders that were since null and void."

"The order to suspend operations was within Administration protocol–"

"The power of the Colonial Expansion Board is moot." Hammond flicked her hand. "And as Mr. Morimoto's Coalition has not officially assumed control, the Project itself is in flux. I, therefore, allowed Mr. Ambri-Cutt to continue his attempts."

The Chairman shouted, "You authorized this... this breach?"

"You knew?" Ambri-Cutt cried.

Hammond fixed him with her gray gaze. "Understand. Nothing happens within my jurisdiction that I don't know about. I did not stop you, so yes–I authorized it."

The Board erupted with shouts.

Hammond's face remained impassive. "I contacted the Coalition and told them that one of my technicians was on the verge of a revolutionary breakthrough, one that would make scouting safer and more public friendly. But even I was amazed to learn that his tracking system actually worked."

"But it didn't work," the Chairman bellowed. "He sent those cadets to their deaths."

She shook her head. "Think. The ring doesn't differentiate between dead and alive. If they had died, their bodies would have returned. But the ring came back empty. The only possible explanation is that the rescuers located the missing cadets and were subsequently carried off by the errant ring."

A hush muffled the room.

Miss Johnston turned to Mr. Ambri-Cutt. "I think you're about to come into a lot of money."

Twilight fell. Impani stood with Trace and Robert, watching the purple-skinned villagers prepare for Joss' luau. The sides of the tower were dismantled and rearranged as long banquet tables. The tower's perch was filled with brush and set on fire. Villagers rushed from their homes carrying baskets of smoked fish and dried fruit. They hooted to one another, eyes downcast.

Impani said, "Do you get the impression that they're giving up their winter stores? None of this food is fresh."

Trace nodded. "They don't look happy."

"Their faces are like rubber," Robert said. "How can you tell if they're happy or not?"

"I can't. But I can tell that using up all your provisions in one night is not smart. Neither is lighting a bonfire during a time of war."

"They're his subjects." Robert jabbed him with his finger. "He's not about to abuse them."

Trace shoved his hand away.

Impani looked again at Joss. The man stood amid the commotion, waving his arms as if conducting an orchestra.

"He said he survived another year," she said. "I wonder how long he's been here."

As if sensing they were speaking about him, Joss looked their way. Impani shuddered. Then two people approached them, braying and pointing. They picked up one end of Natica's branch and dragged her away.

"Hey!" Impani rushed after them. "Be careful with her!"

They stopped at the low table and propped the branch so that Natica sat upright. As if she were going to eat. Impani knelt at her side.

"She's all right." Joss sat on the ground at the head of the table. "Let her sleep."

Impani steadied her friend's lolling head. "You don't understand."

"How dare you disagree with me?" Joss bellowed. "And why are you all so young?"

294

"We're cadets." Trace sat across the table from Impani and Natica. "Our Impellic ring fractured."

Robert sat at Joss' elbow. "I'm the rescue party."

Both he and Joss chuckled.

Impani asked, "Why did you say this was the end of the line?"

"End of the line! End of the line! Sniffle, piffle, mope and whine." Joss cackled insanely. "Let me guess. You've been jumping from planet to planet, and you can't stop, and you can't get back to the Chamber."

"Yes. That's right." Impani leaned forward.

"Well, this is where your adventure finally fizzles. No one has ever ringed off this planet."

Impani's heart dropped. Natica will save them, she told herself. Natica knows what to do with the components.

"There are other Scouts here?" Trace asked.

"Dead. Only Beaumont and I are left. You're the first to come through in a few months."

"Where's Beaumont?" asked Robert.

"Is this an interrogation?" Joss shouted. "Are you spies?"

He scratched madly at his face. Even in the firelight, Impani could see lice hopping around his beard.

"Beaumont lives across the river," he said. "With a different tribe of *grapes*."

"The tribe you're at war with?" she asked.

Joss grinned and gazed over her head. "Here she comes. The guest of honor."

Impani watched two villagers drag a gnarled tree limb from a hut. As they neared, she noticed a body tangled with the branches. It wore a skinsuit.

"This is my partner, Madelia," Joss said as the purple people propped the body to the table. "We jumped to twenty-seven planets before hitting the end of the line. Unfortunately,

Madelia died on the second one. But she kept jumping with me. Everywhere I went. I thought I was being haunted." He slammed his fist against the table and yelled at the suit, "I told you I was sorry!"

Impani felt as if she was at a mad tea party. She stared at the dead Scout. It still wore a utility belt. Grass showed behind its closed mask. "Is Madelia inside her suit?"

"Not anymore." Joss took a metal goblet from a server. "I dumped her bones in the river."

"Is that what the *grapes* do with their dead?" Robert also took a goblet. "Throw them in the river?"

"Them?" Joss chortled. "They don't even have bones. Just gristle and meat. Makes them flexible but not very strong."

More people joined them at the table. They passed around woven plates–like shallow baskets made of grass. Joss heaped his plate with smoked fish and something that looked like dried chili peppers.

Just then, the burning tower collapsed upon itself, sending a shower of sparks into the air.

Joss hooted and waved a fish at the huge bonfire. "Let the entertainment begin!"

Impani heard an arrhythmic thumping. A purple person struck a hollow log with a stick. She didn't think he meant the sound to be music—but several villagers moved nearer the fire to dance. Their arms coiled and writhed like snakes, and their legs bent in too many places.

Joss laughed and pounded the table.

Robert pointed. "Look at that one!"

"Didn't I tell you they were flexible?" He slapped him on the back.

Impani turned from the eerie dance. She sniffed the dark liquid within her goblet. It smelled like turpentine. She returned it to the table. Cautiously, she nibbled a fish, which was chewy, and the pepper, which was sweet.

As she ate, she realized that everyone at the table wore chainmail. In the shadows, naked people gathered with their arms draped about their children, watching the diners.

"Aren't they allowed to eat?" she asked.

"Fighters eat first." Joss smacked his lips. "As in every great society."

"But the children are malnourished," she blurted. "Look at their distended stomachs."

He leaned forward and glared at her. In a voice one would use with a disobedient child, he said, "The *grapes* are marsupials, like opossums or kangaroos. The bloating is just immature pouches."

She felt herself go red. "I thought they were starving."

"We wouldn't let that happen. It would be counterproductive. If we run low on food, Beaumont will send some over, and if he runs low, I'll do the same."

"But aren't you two at war?"

"It's not war." He sniggered. "It's a game. Like a video game. The kind where you get to play god."

"Some game," she muttered. "We saw people die."

He flicked his hand. "Pawns."

Impani stared in appalled silence. She glanced at Trace. His lips were in a tense line. Robert avidly watched the dancers, grinning.

Then Natica stirred and moaned. Her eyelids fluttered.

Impani leaned over her. "Natica? Are you all right?"

Her friend looked up, bleary eyed. "Impani? Where are we?"

Chapter 16

Trace blew out a breath of relief as Natica spoke. She appeared groggy, but that was to be expected. Impani fumbled through her belt then drew out her water flask. He could tell it was empty by the way she looked at it, so he leaned forward and offered his. She paid him a quick smile then held the flask to her friend's lips. Natica sipped and sputtered. She pushed it away.

"We've been so worried," Impani said.

"What happened?" Natica glanced around. "How did I get here?"

Impani looked at Trace as if stricken.

He lowered his voice in what he hoped was a soothing manner. "What's the last thing you remember?"

"I was at breakfast, and Impani was talking about... Trace?" She blinked. "What are you doing here?"

"Breakfast?" Impani cried. "You remember breakfast?"

"It's all right, Impani," Trace said.

"It's not all right!" she cried, her face etched with panic. "What about the components? What about getting us home?"

"Memory lapses are common after a concussion. Perhaps after she—"

"Hey, Galos." Wilde walked around the end of the table. "About time you woke up."

"Robert?" Natica pressed her fingers against her temples. "I don't remember what happened. I don't remember!"

"Calm down," Impani said. "We'll figure everything out."

She moaned. "It hurts to think."

Impani turned to Joss. "Is there a place we can take our friend to rest?"

His face darkened, and he growled, "You're leaving my luau?"

"Regrettably, we must." Trace inclined his head. "Your Highness."

Joss stared at him, his expression stony. Finally, he said, "You can spend the night in the cabana. It will be quieter there."

He hooted, and a boneless person rushed to his side. The villager listened for a moment then motioned to the cadets.

"Can you walk?" Impani asked Natica.

Her friend nodded, but her movements were shaky. Impani supported her with an arm about her waist.

Wilde said, "I think I'll stay. Keep an eye on things here."

"That's a good idea." Impani patted his shoulder. "Find out what you can."

Trace's fists clenched. As if Wilde had any intentions other than to carouse with the natives.

"Thank you, sir." Impani smiled at Joss as she passed.

The Emperor scowled.

They followed their guide into the woods. Natica stumbled over the long grass, so Trace swept her into his arms. Firelight flickered through the trees, lighting their way, and the pounding drumbeat echoed.

However, the farther they went, the quieter it became. A cold, brittle breeze rattled the corkscrew reeds. The trees thinned, and a lake came into view. Its water glimmered beneath a large silver moon.

The purple-skinned alien led them along the bank to a grass hut. Trace carried Natica through the circular doorway then paused in the gloom. He made out a sparse, windowless room. It stank of mildew and fish.

Impani switched on the wrist lamp and stepped around him. "There's something like a bed in the center."

Entering the hut, he placed Natica upon a platform of reeds cushioned with woven grass mats. Natica winced and rubbed her forehead with trembling fingers.

Impani sat on the ground beside her. "How do you feel?"

She moaned. "I keep trying to recall–"

"Don't. Just relax. It will come to you."

"But what if it doesn't? What if I never remember?"

"You will." Impani smiled. "Trace is right. You've had an injury. We can't expect you to remember everything right away."

Trace took out his med-pac. "I'll give you something for the headache." He fed a dose of analgesic to the derma-jecter and pressed it under her chin.

Natica jerked at the pop of the 'jecter.

"Get some sleep." Impani smoothed her friend's brow.

Obediently, Natica closed her eyes. Soon her face relaxed, and her breathing slowed.

Impani motioned to Trace then tiptoed through the door. She glanced around. "Our guide must have gone back to the luau."

"I'm happy to get away from it. Although I was hungry."

"Me, too." She unclipped the flashlight from her wrist. "This is yours."

"Thanks." He hooked it to his belt.

She walked toward the lake. The water was smooth and dark, reflecting the moon like a black mirror. The curly reeds became more numerous.

He said, "Everything grows in spirals on this planet. Reeds, grass, tree branches."

"I kind of like it." She pointed at lights on the shoreline. "What are those? Lanterns?"

"Maybe phosphorescent flowers."

She tossed a smile over her shoulder then led him along the stony bank toward one of the lights. Close up, it looked even more like a flower–a long stem topped with tiny white lights. But as Impani reached for it, the lights broke apart, flying about before again settling on the reed.

"They're moths," she gasped, her eyes alight.

If he lived to be a thousand, he would never forget the look of delight on her face. She waved her fingers to make them fly again.

He pulled her higher upon the bank. They stood hand-in-hand, looking out over the glassy surface of the lake.

"This is a beautiful world," she said, "but–"

"But we don't belong here."

She looked thoughtful for moment then brightened. "But now that Natica is awake–"

"Not so fast. She might not regain her memory all at once."

"She'll remember. She has to."

Trace could almost hear her thoughts continue—*only Natica knows how to save them*. But in the time they'd spent together, he'd learned to trust Impani's instinct, her ingenuity. He knew that if she tried she could put that circuit board together. She could do anything—and he wanted to tell her so.

Instead, he said, "How did you and Wilde get together?"

"He's just a guy." She sat on the bank and tossed a pebble into the water. "Robert isn't so bad, really. He's the only child of Admiral Amanda Wilde."

Trace stared. "Of the Space Corps?"

She nodded. "He joined the Colonial Scouts on a dare. A motherly don't you dare."

She laughed softly. He hadn't heard her laugh in a long while.

Feeling vaguely discomfited, he sat beside her on the rocks. He never had to compete for a girl's attentions before. His family fortune made it simple. But he didn't think Impani would be impressed by land or money.

Finally, he said, "You never did tell me your secret."

❧ ❧ ❧

Impani stiffened. Had he read her thoughts? "I don't know where to begin."

"Start anywhere you like." He draped his arm about her. "If the story needs to be told, it will come out."

He was right, of course. Already she could feel the words bubbling up her throat in a rush to be heard. But how could she explain? How could she make him understand how desperate she was, how alone?

In a low voice, she said, "I studied so hard to get into the program. It was all I thought about, my only means of escape. But when I finally went to the recruitment center, the recruiter told me the Scouts didn't take in every guttersnipe that came along. I was devastated. Humiliated. I never felt so worthless. Then he acted as if he was taking pity on me. He told me that a local gang was scaring recruits away from his door. If I could get him the names of the leaders and where to find them, he would push for my acceptance into the academy." Tears filled her eyes, surprising her. She thought she'd cried them out long ago.

"A dangerous mission," Trace murmured, "infiltrating a street gang."

She shook her head. "They weren't what I expected. They lived in the lower levels of an abandoned shopping mall. There were families there. Like a community. I thought that perhaps I had the wrong place. These people weren't a threat to anyone. But when I made my report, the recruiter just smiled and said that I should wait there and keep my cover. So I waited and actually made some friends. I convinced myself I wasn't betraying them, just giving up the names of their leaders. They would be arrested, probably put in jail."

Her words broke, and she swallowed several times. Her sight turned inward– revisiting the nightmare, living it all again. She saw people running, shadows in smoke, the flash of erupting gunfire.

Trace tightened his arm about her shoulders as if bracing them both.

When she spoke again, she didn't recognize her own voice. "They came in with flamethrowers. Burned them alive. All of them. Women. Children. I remember their screams, the horrible smell of fuel."

"They *burned* them?"

"They didn't give them a chance. Oh, God." She covered her face. "I didn't mean for it to happen."

"You were still there?"

She nodded and wiped her eyes. "He meant for me to die along with them. You should have seen his face when I showed up at the recruitment center. When I accused him of murder, he said he meant it as a show of force, a statement to the other gang leaders who wanted him out of their area. He actually expected to be heralded a hero for cleaning up the neighborhood, never understood the public outcry."

"I'm surprised the public even learned of it," Trace said.

"I turned him in." A quavering sigh escaped her. "There was a trial. Everyone knew what had happened."

"You risked everything."

"I couldn't live with what I'd done. Unfortunately, the other gangs feel the same way. I'll be killed if I don't make the program."

"Suddenly, my stint in a penal colony looks pretty pale."

"After the scandal died down, the CEB assigned a new recruiter to the center. He was once a Scout himself. He told me that cadets are accepted on merit, not in exchange for money or information." She grimaced. "How could I let myself be used like that?"

"Impani, I–"

"I don't deserve to be a Scout."

"You'll make a great Scout. I've never been paired with anyone better. And there's no one I'd rather be lost with."

She gave a small chuckle then sniffled. "On the ant world, when we were in that storage shed, you were about to kiss me. Why didn't you?"

"You were frightened, and I didn't want you to look back and think I had taken advantage."

"I'm not frightened anymore." She looked up at him.

He held her gaze, his deep eyes shadowed. Gently, he cupped her face in his hands. A blush warmed her cheeks. She touched his shoulder, drawing him closer.

A shriek rent the air.

Impani bolted upright. "That's Natica."

Trace leaped to his feet then ran along the bank, boots skittering upon the rocks. Impani followed, ears sharpened for sound, eyes wide in the black night. They reached the silent hut. Trace played his flashlight over the clearing and the surrounding brush, one hand upon his gun. Impani rushed past him, diving through the doorway.

Natica sat upon the narrow bed. She trembled visibly, and her face glistened with sweat in the faint light. "You're here. I thought I dreamed you. I thought I was alone."

Impani hugged her. "It's all right. I won't leave again."

"I don't know what's happening to me."

"You'll feel better in the morning. You'll take one look at those circuit chips and—"

"But you don't understand," Natica wailed. "It's not like it's a name that's on the tip of my tongue. It's not as if I know I should remember something but I'm drawing a blank. No time has passed for me. We had breakfast and then I was here."

Impani held her close, rocking her gently as she wept. What if Natica never remembered? How would they get back to the academy?

Trace peered through the doorway. Impani stared at him, unable to speak. She imagined spending her life on this world, living under Joss' delusional godhood.

She had to do something.

Chapter 17

Trace woke slowly from dreams about flamethrowers. He opened his eyes to the gray light of morning, at first not knowing where he was. Then he remembered forming a bed out of the grass floor in the back of the hut.

He rolled over and gazed at the sunlight seeping through the roof. Joss' cabana was in disrepair. He studied the thinning patches of vegetation above him. A grid-like frame of reeds showed through swirls of stringy grass— architecture different from the wooden tower in the middle of the village. Would this culture have considered cutting down trees for lumber if Emperor Joss and his counterparts hadn't intruded upon them?

He sat up and rubbed his face. His gloves smelled as musty as his bed. Natica slept upon the platform in the center of the room. With a start, he realized Impani wasn't there. He rushed from the hut and found her outside with the components strewn before her.

He let out a breath and knelt. "Good morning."

She showed him the board. "Take a look at this. Does it seem familiar?"

"It's like the homing device in your belt buckle. Only larger."

"I think Robert is right. It gives us the ability to call an Impellic ring."

"What good is that if the ring's still fractured?"

"That's where these chips come in." She snapped a small board onto the edge of the larger. "I think they're meant to modify the signal once we're actually inside the ring, re-directing energy from the healthy rings onto the broken one."

"Stabilizing it until we can get through."

"The problem is I don't know the proper configuration. Their edges are color coded, but the motherboard is not."

"Match it to the device inside your buckle."

"I tried." She motioned at her belt lying in the grass. "It's all integrated. I can't get the parts off the board to look at them."

He watched her in silence. He could almost see thoughts racing behind her bright eyes.

"The academy knows we aren't techs. They would try to keep the device as simple as possible." She rattled the chips in her hand then tossed them down. "I wish I had another belt for comparison."

"Well, here. Take mine."

"No," she yelped. "We can't risk damaging it. What if this isn't the end of the line."

"You think we might be picked up even after what Joss said?"

"We can only hope."

Trace nodded. He didn't want to stay on this world any more than she did. "What about Joss' partner? Her suit had a belt."

"That's right. I wonder if the Royal Emperor would let us have it."

"One way to find out." He stood. "Be right back."

She caught his hand. "Be careful. I don't trust Joss."

No doubt. The man's a maniac. Interesting how easily Wilde fit in with him. Trace grinned. "Don't worry."

A well-trampled path cut through the trees. It was easier to follow in daylight. As he walked, he glanced skyward and realized that this was the first wooded planet he'd visited that didn't have birds. He studied the bent and twisted branches, noticing only a few small mammals. Then the pungent smell of smoke reached him. Was the bonfire still burning?

The forest opened onto the village. Trace froze, staring. People sprawled over the tables, upon the ground, around the smoking ruins of the lookout tower. At first, he thought they were dead, that the village had been attacked while he slept in the cabana. Then he noticed other people moving in and out of the huts, hooting quietly to one another as if the scene were as natural as anything else was on this world.

Not dead. Inebriated. On the brew that was in the goblets.

Stepping carefully around the revelers, he approached the main table. Joss sat with his face in a plate. Wilde lay slumped to the side. Trace nudged him with his boot.

"Huh? What?" Wilde looked about, eyes unfocused.

"I hope you gathered some good intel on this place," Trace said.

Wilde scowled and held his head. "Suck eggs, Hanson."

"What's that?" Joss boomed. "You came back? How did you enjoy the cabana?"

"Fine, sir. Nice view."

"Never go there, myself. Smells like fish." He guffawed. "Let me show you around my empire."

He clasped Trace's shoulder, leaning heavily upon him as he walked. Trace cringed from the stench of the man's breath.

Joss pointed. "There's a hut, and there's a hut. And there's my royal palace. From this angle it kind of looks like a hut."

He laughed and slapped Trace's back. Wilde glared murderously and stepped to Joss' other side.

"How long have you been here, sir?" Trace asked.

"This location? Not that long." Joss stroked his matted beard. "The *grapes* used to be nomads, following the migration of fish. But I don't like all that moving around. So I introduced fire and taught them how to smoke fish and wait out the winter months. Then Beaumont came along." Chuckling, he returned to the table, pried a goblet out of a sleeping warrior's hand, and drank deeply.

Trace watched. How would he bring the topic around to his partner's belt?

Wilde stepped toward Joss. "What did Beaumont do?"

"He taught his side how to use my fire to smelt ore and make spearheads," Joss said. "I countered with chainmail, of course."

"Why didn't you just use stat-guns? You must have inherited a few."

"Six, actually. But we decided early on that using tech would be cheating."

Wilde grinned and sat cross-legged on the table. "What you need is an old-fashioned hammerhead slug pistol."

"Yeah, but this planet's got drel for resources," Joss said. "No way to make gunpowder. No crude or kerosene."

Wilde nodded. "I see the challenge."

"The last thing Beaumont brought was hot air balloons. I tried arrows to bring them down, but the *grapes* have no upper-body strength. So I devised a crossbow with rapid load." Joss removed a crossbow from one of the warrior's wrists and held it out to Wilde.

Wilde whistled. "Nice workmanship."

Trace said, "Sir, could I borrow Madelia's belt?"

"What do you want with it?" Joss asked without looking up.

"We want to open the buckle and compare the homing device with what we have. We're trying to construct a new device that will—"

"You're building a homer?" Joss laughed, shaking his head. "Kids."

Trace pulled back his shoulders. "Yes, sir."

Joss looked him up and down. Suddenly he leaped onto the table and crowed like a rooster. The sleeping warriors stirred. Villagers rushed from the huts. Joss honked and hooted, waving his arms and kicking goblets into the air.

Trace watched with feigned calm, stifling the urge to step out of the way. Wilde sat stiffly on the table as if afraid to move.

Then Joss knocked over his partner's effigy and stripped the belt from the suit. He grinned at Trace, his eyes wide and mad. "Show me." Turning sharply, he goose-stepped across the village.

"Are you crazy?" Wilde whispered. "He already told you that you can't ring off this planet. You're throwing it in his face."

"I'm crazy?" Trace hissed back. "How do you deal with someone like that? One minute he's lucid, the next he's out of control."

"He rules here." With a knowing nod, Wilde followed Joss into the trees.

Trace hurried to keep up. "He's a madman. And he's destroying this culture."

"What are you talking about?"

"This war of his against Beaumont. These people aren't killers. They make their homes out of living grass."

"So he taught them a thing or two."

They entered the path leading to the cabana. Ahead, Joss cackled and marched, cracking the belt like a whip.

Trace cringed with apprehension. Lowering his voice, he said, "A true leader would be benevolent."

"Benevolent?" Wilde sneered. "No ruler has ever been benevolent. You can't pander to others and expect them to do your bidding at the same time."

"But to alter an entire society—"

"Watch yourself, Hanson. Joss should be admired for all he's accomplished. In any case, he's our one hope for survival on this planet."

Trace snapped his mouth shut and fell back a few paces. Wilde was as deluded as his emperor. Perhaps after Impani connected the components, they should leave the two of them behind.

🪐 🪐 🪐

Impani sat outside the cabana, speaking quietly to Natica. "And then you fell into the crevice left by the lightning bolt."

"How long was I unconscious?"

"I don't know. The better part of a day, I guess. I was beginning to–" She looked toward the sound of singing coming from the trees. "Oh, no. The emperor is here."

Joss stepped from the forest path, twirling a belt overhead and giving an off-key rendition of *The Farmer in the Dell.* Trace and Robert followed. Trace appeared anxious, waving for her attention behind Joss' back.

Joss did a jig along the outskirts of the clearing, singing, "The rat took the cheese."

Trace mouthed *put them away*.

Impani frowned, perplexed. Then she gathered the components and scooped them into their package.

"The cheese stands alone," Joss sang loudly, leaning over her.

Impani stammered, "G-good m-morning, Your Honor."

"Whatcha got there, little girl?" Joss asked.

"Electronic components." She rose to her feet. "Circuit chips."

He wiggled his fingers, silently demanding the package.

She glanced at Trace then handed over the components. "We're trying to put together a controlling device to summon an Impellic ring. But the chips are color coded and–"

"Industry standard," he said, peering inside.

She stared at him. "What?"

"Techs use a common denominator to make components interchangeable. These are standard colors."

It was as if a bomb went off in Impani's mind. Images assailed her, and she struggled to make sense of them.

Trace said, "But in what order?"

"It's a set pattern." Joss shrugged.

Impani closed her eyes. She pictured Missus hunched over the control box on the ant planet. The motherboard looked like a rainbow. She saw it in her mind as clearly as if she had taken a holograph.

"So what is the pattern?" Trace asked, his voice rising.

Joss laughed. "How should I know? I'm not a tech."

"Orange, yellow, green, blue, black, white, red," Impani said. She snatched the parcel from Joss' hands and poured it onto the ground, laying the chips in order. Elation filled her. She glanced at the blank faces staring down at her. "Red and white connect the power, so they must go on the end here." She snapped the chips onto the motherboard.

"You'll never do it." Joss snickered. "Greater minds than yours have tried to find a way off this world. You're just a kid."

"There's room for three along this side," Natica murmured.

"Even if you do call a ring," Joss said, "which of you will be leaving? You know it can carry only two."

"That's not quite right, sir," Robert cooed sycophantically. "The four of us came here in the same ring."

Trace said, "Impani and I once carried an animal between worlds."

"A large animal." Impani smirked at Joss. "So if I can get this thing working, you can come back with us."

Joss stared. "Me?"

"Sure. Don't you want to finally leave this planet?"

His face melted into a slow grin. "It would be one hell of a debriefing."

Impani reached for her belt and opened the buckle. A line of lights blinked merrily. She paused. "Wait. The power crystal is integrated. It won't detach. I need a separate power supply."

"Hello?" Robert sang out. "The power pack is missing."

Trace knelt. "Can you use a stat-gun like you did for Missus?"

She shook her head. "The proton beam of a stat-gun is powered by static electricity converted from the air. There's no air inside a wormhole."

Robert cried, "Why can't you just listen to me?"

"Why can't you be a little more supportive?" Trace snapped.

"There must be something we can use." Natica glanced from person to person.

Impani frowned, her head too full to think. Then her gaze fell upon the belt in Joss' hand. "The resonator. Madelia had a resonator. Joss, let me see that belt."

Joss handed her his partner's belt. She took out the resonator and flipped it open. Dusty lights flitted across the face.

"It's still charged." She flashed a smile at the silent group. Beneath the pressure of their stares, she slid back the case. A removable power pack sat amid red-and-white connectors. She opened her own resonator and pulled out a length of wire. "I think I can daisy-chain them together."

"Take mine, too." Robert shrugged. "We might need the extra energy."

She smiled and nodded. It took only a few moments to strip the packs and attach them in line to each other.

As she finished, she said, "The only way this will work is if everyone holds onto me."

Joss sniffed. "Not a secure mode of travel."

Impani stood with the device in one hand and the linked power packs in the other. She took a deep breath and nodded. "Here we go."

Chapter 18

With trembling fingers, Impani plugged the power packs into the motherboard. Immediately, the board vibrated with an almost inaudible hum. A whirling sensation stirred her stomach.

Joss whooped and crushed her in a bear hug. "The ring is coming! We're on our way!"

Trace wrapped one arm about her shoulders and held Natica with the other. Robert held onto her waist. Impani closed her eyes, willing the device to work.

The ring never arrived.

"What happened?" Robert asked.

Impani shrugged from the group embrace. "Not enough power." She disconnected the unit.

"But we're almost there," Trace told her. "You put the components together. You figured it out."

Suddenly, she wanted to cry. "What good does it do if we can't make it work?"

Joss burst into gales of laughter. She glowered, caught between embarrassment and indignation.

"Don't leave without me," he chortled and ran into the trees.

"Where's he going?" Robert asked.

Natica shook her head.

"Who cares?" Impani's gaze dropped to the board in her hand. "Joss is right. I'll never do it."

"But you *have* done it." Trace cupped her chin. "I felt the ring."

"I didn't feel anything," Robert said, sullenly.

Trace shoved him. "Joss felt it."

"Joss is crazy!" Impani cried.

"So what are you going to do?" Trace asked. "Give up?"

"At least we're on a hospitable world," Robert said. "Joss has lived here for two years."

"And what happened to the other Scouts who landed here?" Trace glared at him. "Did you ever wonder about that?"

"They died of parasites." Robert lowered his voice. "The *grapes* call it the children's disease—little worms that eat you from the inside. Joss said it's a long and gruesome death."

"Great," Natica said.

"This is hopeless." Impani let the board fall from her hand. It sank into the grass. For a moment, they all stared at it. She felt like she was at a funeral.

Then Robert screwed up his face. "Do you hear yodeling?"

Head cocked, Impani led the group across the clearing. She stared down the village path. Joss walked briskly toward them, yodeling at the top of his lungs. He carried an armful of equipment belts over one shoulder.

The belts from the other Scouts. Joss hadn't meant to ridicule her—he'd gone for more power packs. She clamped her lips tight against a swell of renewed hope. Did she dare try again? The others looked to her to save them. What if she failed?

She hung her head, wishing that her friends weren't standing so close behind her, wishing she had time to think. But an odd sound stole her concentration—a discordant, multi-leveled buzz. It took a moment to realize what it was.

The villagers were screaming.

Silvery bubbles settled over the forest, bobbing as if tethered. Thin fingers of smoke wavered in the air. Then a silver hot air balloon cleared the trees behind Joss.

She cried, "Look out!"

Joss turned as the balloon sped toward him. A man leaned low over the basket's edge and pitched a fist-sized glass ball. It struck Joss in the chest. Immediately, flames engulfed him. Joss dove to the ground, the belts flying.

Impani cringed. The skinsuit wouldn't burn— but his beard would. She rushed forward to help him.

Robert pulled her back. "I'll handle it." He ran down the path.

A soldier in the basket threw out an anchor that tangled in the trees. The balloon bobbed in place.

"Hello, Joss," the man called. "I finally found a use for fish oil." He wore a skinsuit and a handlebar mustache. Beaumont. He held out another ball. It looked like a Christmas ornament with a wick.

Joss extinguished the flames by rolling on the ground. Smoke curled from his beard.

Robert reached him and helped him up. He tugged Joss' arm, but he wrenched it away.

"Molotov cocktails?" he yelled at Beaumont. "Not very original."

Beaumont laughed so hard he nearly fell out of the basket. "What's the matter? Can't keep up?"

Joss hooted and shook his fist. Both men grinned. Beaumont released the balloon and drifted over the lake.

Looking disgruntled, Robert gathered the belts. He said something to Joss.

Joss leaped up and down, yelling, "I can't go yet. The game isn't over." With a hoarse battle cry, he ran toward the village.

Robert gaped. Was he finally seeing that Joss was insane? Or was he deciding whether or not to go with him?

The voices of the villagers grew louder. Crashing footsteps sounded in the woods. The balloons once tethered over the village moved steadily nearer. One followed the path toward Robert, dipping low enough for two soldiers to jump from the basket. They brandished long swords.

Robert pulled out his stat-gun and fired at the ground in front of them, gouging a black gully. "Just cross the line!" he yelled. "Go ahead!"

The soldiers collided in an attempt to back away–but the balloon kept coming. The lone balloonist tossed several flaming balls overboard. They fell nowhere near Robert–but he fired anyway.

Robert's shot crackled in arcs over the metal-foil balloon. The ropes that attached the wicker basket snapped. With a strident screech, the balloonist fell into the trees.

"Robert, no," Impani cried. "We aren't here to butcher the–"

She stopped at the sight of another balloon. Its occupants peppered the cabana with glass balls as if hoping to flush someone out. Smoke rose from the grass roof.

"The circuit boards." She headed toward the cabana.

Trace grabbed her arm. He pulled her back just as a mob of villagers burst from the trees. The three cadets huddled together, tossed and jostled as the panicked crowd streamed around them. Balloons bobbed overhead, and soldiers leaped from them as if impervious to harm.

Impani covered her ears then yelled to Trace. "Get Natica to safety!"

He looked startled. "But—"

"I have to get the components before they're trashed." She pushed him away and entered the mayhem.

For a moment, all she saw was purple skin and white hair, all she heard was a roar—and she felt like she were back again in the frothing rapids. She bounded from body to body, fighting her way crosscurrent as the villagers stampeded blindly toward the lake. Then Trace was beside her, shouldering the people away, and keeping her from falling beneath their pounding feet.

Together, they pushed through to the cabana. Smoke poured from the door. Flames crackled inside. Impani searched for the circuit board–and found it kicked against the side of the hut, chips askew.

"Any damage?" Trace shouted.

"I hope not." She scooped the fallen chips into their package. "Where's Natica?"

"With Wilde."

An arrow whizzed past his ear. He yelped then turned to shield her.

Like a tsunami, Joss' warriors surged from the trees and engulfed Beaumont's soldiers. The air rang with the clash of swords against chainmail. Arrows flew, finding their mark in throats and torsos. Within moments, the clearing filled with bodies.

"This is insane," Impani cried.

Trace leaned close and yelled, "We have to get to the others across the clearing."

"How?"

As if in answer, he secured his mask. Impani did the same. She stared at the teeming warriors as they hacked and grappled and died. There was no path through them. No way across. Then at her back, the cabana collapsed in a flurry of sparks.

"Drel!" She leaped away.

A warrior careened into her, his rubbery face sliced nearly in two. She screamed and batted him to the side.

Trace shook her shoulders. "Do you have everything?"

"What?"

"The circuit board."

She blinked then searched the package. "Yes. I think so."

He took out his gun. "Follow me."

Together, they rushed into the melee. Bodies littered the ground. Some trampled to death–others hacked to pieces. Beaumont's soldiers wielded their swords deftly. One came after her and Trace.

"Stay away!" Trace pointed the stat-gun.

The soldier charged them, sword high overhead. Trace fired. But instead of striking the person, he shot the sword, causing less damage. A wave of love washed through Impani. They weren't there to butcher the locals.

The metal sword glowed bright white. The soldier twitched convulsively, but he would not release the weapon. Impani whirled about and landed a solid kick on his chest. He flew backward and landed in a heap.

Trace grabbed her arm and pulled her forward. A volley of arrows rained over them. She looked back as warriors shot straight up in the air, trying to hit the hovering balloons. One arrow reached its target. The silvery foil tore, and the basket plummeted. With a braying sound, Joss' warriors stormed the balloonist.

"Come on!" Trace tugged her, and she realized she'd been almost stationary, mired in horror.

Ahead, Robert and Natica beckoned from the village path. Head bent against a torrent of arrows, she sprinted toward them.

Robert caught her. "Are you all right?"

"We have to get out of here," she cried.

Trace asked, "Has Joss shown up?"

"That loony." Robert glanced down the path. "When we get home, we'll send someone back for him."

When we get home. The words echoed against Impani's misgivings. She straightened. "Where are the belts?"

"We've got three more power packs." Robert handed her the resonators. "The others are depleted."

"Let's hope it's enough," said Natica.

"It will be." *It has to be.*

Impani carried the components and the resonators deeper into the trees, away from the battle. Sitting in a flattened area of grass, she examined the circuit chips for damage then clipped them back into place.

Natica said, "Maybe Joss was right about this not being a secure way to travel. I mean, just holding onto one another–"

"Impani, remember when we connected our belts to secure that creature to the sled?" Trace said. "Maybe if we join these extra belts, we can strap the four of us together."

"Do it," Impani said without looking up.

She linked two of the packs in line with the others–but the third was so old, its connector crumbled. She had to hotwire it into the chain. At last, she got to her feet.

"Ready?" she asked.

"Done." Trace dragged the string of belts.

Natica moved to Impani's side. Eyes wide. Lips tight.

Impani gave her an encouraging smile. "Hold onto me, just in case."

"Look," Robert said. "The village is burning."

A dirty smudge rose over the trees.

"I won't miss this world," she murmured.

"Me neither." He fastened his mask then draped his arms over the girls' shoulders.

Trace wrapped the belts about them and snapped the buckle shut. He faced Impani. "It's up to you now."

Time to take a chance. She plugged the power coupling into the board.

Immediately, a familiar tug grasped the pit of her stomach. Darkness formed within her mind. She imagined a circle of swirling black energy, sensed tendrils reaching toward her, pulling her from the world on which she stood.

It was working! They had summoned an Impellic ring. For a moment, she felt faint. She concentrated on the nearness of her friends, their arms about her, supporting her. The void took hold—deep and empty yet giving the impression of extreme velocity.

Then blinding light speared her eyes. She winced into the glare. Her vision wavered then focused upon a mirrored room.

The Impellic Chamber.

"We did it!" Robert yelled. "We're back!"

Natica bounced up and down, causing the belts to fall to the floor.

Trace cupped Impani's face in his palms, his deep eyes luminous. "You are amazing."

Impani gasped, not yet willing to trust her voice, not yet certain she should believe.

Then the door burst open, and a man she recognized as Chief Astrut rushed into the Chamber. He gaped at them.

Impani grinned. "We're ready for our debriefing."

Chapter 19

Impani held Trace's hand as they walked toward the door to Natica's hospital room. She felt a twinge of guilt. They had been back for a day, yet this was the first chance she'd had to visit her friend. It wasn't her fault, really. The debriefing had been long, and then she'd slept nearly twelve hours while the medical staff pumped fluids into her. She must have needed the rest; she felt much stronger now.

Taking a deep breath, she pushed open the door. Natica sat in bed with her back to them, staring out a circular window at a fading sunset. Her smooth scalp showed a large purple splotch. Impani was relieved to see her sitting up. When she heard that Natica hadn't been released from the hospital, she imagined tubes and monitors, and her friend lying listlessly among them.

"How are you feeling?" Impani approached the bed.

Natica looked about as if she'd been deep in thought. She smiled then gave a mock groan. "Terrible. They want to keep me here another two days. I'll miss graduation."

"You won't be any less a Scout."

"That's quite a bump you've got." Trace smiled. "I think the skinsuit was the only thing keeping your head on tight."

Natica chuckled. "How did you two check out?"

"A few bruises, a bit dehydrated." Impani shrugged. "Nothing serious."

"I still can't believe that out of the four of us Robert was the only one to contract those worms," Natica said. "He'll be in ICU until the doctors figure a way to flush them from his system."

Impani caught Trace's eye, and they smiled.

"You should have been at the debriefing," she said. "Strangest thing I ever saw."

Trace laughed. "Yeah, now that we're privately funded, the interviewers asked all sorts of personal questions. How do we feel about this? How could that have been handled better?"

"They actually wanted your opinion?"

"They want to make scouting safer."

"We told them about Joss and Beaumont," Impani said. "They're going to send a retrieval squad."

"They need to do more than that." Natica leaned back against her pillows. "Those poor people are killing each other, and I bet they don't even know why."

Impani nodded. Would their culture return to normal after two years of Joss' interference? Someone should be accountable. Abruptly, she thought about Missus and the colonists holding the Scouts responsible for their situation.

Quietly, she said, "We also told them about a group of miners we found on an ant world."

Natica blinked. "Ant world?"

"Horrible. I'll tell you about it some time." Then she brightened. "But you'll never guess who was at the debriefing."

"Mr. Ambri-Cutt. I know." Natica laughed. "He came by to thank me for goading him into the rescue. I couldn't bear to tell him that I don't remember doing it."

"You still don't remember anything?"

"Bits and pieces." Natica plucked at her bed sheets. "I remember being in the auditorium. I was crying. And Robert was there, furious that they had suspended operations." She looked at Impani. "He really cares about you, you know."

Impani scoffed. "Obsessed is more like it."

Natica smiled mischievously. "Right. So you can pair up with Robert, and I can go with Trace."

"I'm taken." Trace held up his hands, laughing.

Natica laughed, too. Impani felt her cheeks redden. She was happier at that moment than ever before in her life.

"I think the four of us are going to be too busy to worry about who goes out with whom," she said. "We're Scouts now."

"I like the sound of that," Natica said.

"In the meantime, you'd better get some rest," Impani told her. "We'll be back to see you tomorrow."

"Goodnight," said Trace.

Natica nodded. Trace and Impani stepped out into the hallway, closing the door quietly.

Once out of earshot, she poked Trace in the ribs. "What's all this about you being taken?"

"You know I am," Trace said. "By you."

"But we haven't even kissed."

He stopped walking and placed his hands upon her shoulders. "I've wanted to kiss you since the time I bumped into you in the doorway of the Astrophysics Lab."

She gave a little gasp. "I remember that."

"Those three days we spent lost in that wormhole were right up there with the worst of my life. But they were wonderful, too. Because I got to spend them with you."

Leaning forward, he brushed her cheek with his lips, teasing. She lifted her face toward his. Softly, his lips closed over hers. His kiss was warm and gentle, as she knew him to be, and she found herself wishing it would go on forever. When he pulled away, she looked up at him dreamily.

"Now, you're taken," she whispered.

Read These Other Books

by Roxanne Smolen

The Amazing Wolf Boy

A bumbling nerd becomes a werewolf.

The Amazing Wolf Boy

Werewolf Asylum

Wolfsbane Brew

Werewolf Apocalypse

Dark Angel

A woman breaks into hell to save her daughter.

Satan's Mirror

Dear Reader,

Thank you for reading *Alien Worlds, Colonial Scouts Book 1*. I appreciate your support more than I can tell you. In this age of self-publication, good books can fall to obscurity and never receive the attention they deserve.

That's where you come in. I urge you to leave a brief review at Amazon, Goodreads, or even on your blog. You have the power. I hope you will wield it. And I hope you will look for other books in the Colonial Scouts series.

Sincerely,
Roxanne
www.roxannesmolen.com

www.ingramcontent.com/pod-product-compliance
Lightning Source LLC
Chambersburg PA
CBHW062008170626
46813CB00001B/82